THE PERSEPHONE STAR

JAMIE SULLIVAN

Riptide Publishing
PO Box 1537
Burnsville, NC 28714
www.riptidepublishing.com

This is a work of fiction. Names, characters, places, and incidents are either the product of the author's imagination or are used fictitiously. Any resemblance to actual persons living or dead, business establishments, events, or locales is entirely coincidental. All person(s) depicted on the cover are model(s) used for illustrative purposes only.

The Persephone Star
Copyright © 2016, 2020 by Jamie Sullivan

Cover art: Aisha Akeju
Editor: Carole-ann Galloway
Typography and Layout: L.C. Chase, lcchase.com

All rights reserved. No part of this book may be reproduced or transmitted in any form or by any means, electronic or mechanical, including photocopying, recording, or by any information storage and retrieval system without the written permission of the publisher, and where permitted by law. Reviewers may quote brief passages in a review. To request permission and all other inquiries, contact Riptide Publishing at the mailing address above, at Riptidepublishing.com, or at marketing@riptidepublishing.com.

ISBN: 978-1-62649-931-7

Second edition
February, 2020

Also available in ebook:
ISBN: 978-1-62649-930-0

The Persephone Star

JAMIE SULLIVAN

For S.C.

TABLE OF CONTENTS

I.	1
II.	9
III.	21
IV.	29
V.	37
VI.	47
VII.	57
VIII.	65
IX.	81
X.	91
XI.	97
XII.	107
XIII.	113
XIV.	119
XV.	129
XVI.	139
XVII.	145
XVIII.	151
XIX.	159
XX.	165

The rumors had been flying for days. The ship had been spotted just over the town line, in Copper Creek. It hung heavy in the sky, a blot against the sun, and messages had been streaming into Fortuna's Post Office, warnings and pleas alike.

Penelope took them down dutifully, listening to the clicks of the telegraph and writing the messages in careful, clear letters. She sorted them methodically, pretending that she was merely a conduit for the words that flew over the line, merely another cog in the machine, her pencil connected to the wire that snaked its way through the sky, all part of the great Line.

As postmistress, she knew everyone's business—often before they did. Every family emergency, every business deal gone good or bad. Every love letter sent over the line arrived at its destination in her neat, careful handwriting and every Dear John letter came the same way.

Penelope had to pretend not to see, because she had to look the townspeople in the eye, had to smile at them in the general store, chat with them over coffee at church, dine with them at her father's house. She had to be a townsperson like everyone else, as if she wasn't so full of secrets she often felt liable to burst at the seams, nothing holding her together but the corset that bound her rib cage tight.

So she wrote down the messages from Copper Creek and pretended not to see them, pretended fear didn't well up in her throat as she wrote the name *Mirage Currier* over and over again, and put them in a neat little pile to be delivered to the sheriff.

Tobias Combes came in at midday, looking spooked. He was a frail man, tall but so lean he looked like he'd fall over with a gentle breeze. He crossed his spindly arms on the high counter and bent forward, eyes wide. "A rider just arrived from Copper Creek." He pitched his voice low, as if they weren't the only two in the office.

"Oh?" Penelope said mildly. She knew what he wanted. People came by all the time, "just to chat," knowing Penelope knew more than she let on, hoping she'd let something slip.

She took pride in her job and so kept her lips sealed tight. No one was going to say a woman couldn't be trusted with the line while Penelope was in charge.

"A ship's come into Copper Creek," Tobias continued, his thin face more pinched than usual. "An *outlaw* ship."

If she weren't so unnerved herself, Penelope would have laughed. Everything sounded ridiculous coming from Tobias, a man who could be frightened by a black cat crossing his path.

"Is their sheriff doing anything about it?" Penelope asked. She'd been wondering all day. Surely the problem was Copper Creek's—not theirs.

"They're not causing any trouble, so the sheriff can't do nothing."

"Outlaws who don't cause trouble?" Penelope arched a brow, reaching for the mail sack for something to do with her hands.

"Not in Copper Creek," Tobias said darkly. He bent closer. "It's the *Persephone Star*—Mirage Currier's ship."

Penelope had only been in town for nine months, since her father came to Fortuna to open the town's first bank. But everyone in Fortuna knew the *Persephone Star*—it had become legend, along with its captain, Mirage Currier. Penelope was sure that the legend had spread far beyond their little town. She couldn't believe they weren't talking about it all the way back east. A woman bandit, leading a crew of female outlaws.

"I thought Currier was in jail," Penelope said, forcing blandness into her voice.

"Got out, got her crew together, and came right here."

"To Copper Creek," Penelope corrected.

"For now." Tobias's brows lowered, and Penelope was glad she didn't have to upset him more, to tell him what the messages that had been streaming in all day said: Currier was gathering supplies, trading for guns and ammunition with the worst Copper Creek had to offer. Gearing up to come to Fortuna.

"Don't worry," she said, trying to be kind. "The sheriff will handle it."

"It's him they're coming for," Tobias mumbled, and Penelope turned from the counter, pretending not to hear.

"You mind letting Mrs. Cranshaw know she's got a letter here, Tobias? I know she's been waiting."

"Oh. Course, Miss Moser." Tobias was too polite to stay when he'd been so clearly dismissed. He shuffled out of the office, rolling his narrow shoulders to avoid cracking his head on the doorframe.

Penelope picked up the stack of messages for the sheriff. Everyone knew why Currier was back in town: it was Fortuna's sheriff who had put her away. The *Star* had been terrorizing the good God-fearing folks of the area for too long, and when Wiley got elected sheriff, he'd decided to do something about it. Currier hadn't ever hit Fortuna, but Wiley got together with some of the other sheriffs in the territory and went after her—before she could come after Fortuna, he said.

And now she was back for revenge.

Penelope tucked the sheriff's messages into her knapsack and set about tidying the office for the day. Mail and telegrams got sorted into neat slots under the desk, and the moneybox was kept under lock and key in a safe to be extra secure. Penelope wasn't a fool, and she knew that the post office was the place most likely to be robbed if anyone looking for trouble came to Fortuna.

Once those chores were done, Penelope turned to her pride and joy: the library.

It was really just two shelves on the wall behind the counter, lined with volumes donated by townspeople. But each one had a slip pasted into the front, with neat little boxes to write a due date in.

Only, Penelope couldn't get anyone to borrow them. She'd taken the position as postmistress for something to do, some way to pass the time in the tiny town fate had brought her to. The library was her pet project. She'd been to the public library in New York once, a massive building with stacks and stacks of books for anyone to read. Wandering through, running her childish fingers over the endless spines, Penelope had got it into her head that it was where she belonged. She looked at the women behind the big desks, helping people to find books, and decided then and there that that was what she was going to do when she grew up.

But her father kept them moving, farther and farther west, out of the country and into the territories, and then beyond, into Indian country and the true Wild West. He founded banks in town after town, none of them with libraries.

It was only here, in Fortuna, that Penelope decided to stop wishing and to make her dream happen. If she couldn't move to a town with a library, she could damn well found a library in her town.

For now, there were a dozen books that no one but Penelope had ever bothered to read. She adjusted them on the shelf, lining up the spines neatly and brushing off any dust that had settled over the course of the day.

Turning the heavy key in the lock was her last task of the day, and Penelope smiled with pride at the tidy office before she turned down the street toward her father's house. The summer sun still blazed high in the sky at this hour, making Penelope perspire under the layers of her cotton dress and heavy undergarments.

She ran a self-conscious hand over her face, hoping sweat wasn't beading on her forehead. She offered a smile to the people she passed in the street, waving to the schoolteacher and nodding politely at the reverend as he passed on his way home from church.

Penelope paused outside the house she occupied with her father and straightened her clothes and hair, smoothing any unruly curls back into place in the knot at the back of her head. Taking a deep breath, she squared her shoulders and pasted on a cheerful smile.

Voices rose from within as she stepped through the front door. The girl who did the cleaning met her in the hall with her ever-present anxious smile.

"Anything I can get you, ma'am?"

"No, thank you, Sarah."

Penelope didn't like having servants, not even this teenager, but her father insisted since Penelope wasn't willing to "do her duty" by keeping house for him. Penelope knew she'd be trapped in a man's house soon enough; she didn't want to start just yet.

"Your father and the sheriff are in the parlor," Sarah said with a bobbing curtsy.

Penelope reinforced her smile, and walked down the hall. Her father lounged in his favorite chair, a cigar in his mouth and a whiskey in his hand. Across from him sat Wiley Barnett, his hat on the table in front of him and his sheriff's badge gleaming proudly on his chest.

They both looked up as Penelope paused in the doorway, Wiley's eyes sliding proprietarily over her. Penelope flushed under his gaze, dropping her eyes to hunt through her satchel. Wiley was a handsome man, with hair dark enough to belong to one of the surrounding tribes, and the kind of cocky smile that won people over instantly. He wore the heavy moustache of a military man.

"I brought your telegrams from the office," she said, holding out the stack. Wiley's fingers brushed hers as he took the papers, a lingering stroke over the back of her hand. She fought the urge to pull back, reminding herself that it was allowed. Expected even.

After all, he was her fiancé.

She perched on the sofa as Wiley sorted through the messages with a snort.

"Lot of telegrams," Ashes observed. Her father had the bulk of a man of his station, the buttons of his waistcoat straining over his thick waist. He raised his eyebrows expectantly, waiting to be told all the secrets Wiley held in his hand.

Wiley raised his head, a hard, amused look in his light eyes. "All from Copper Creek. Probably funded their post office for a year with these." He tossed the stack down on the table in front of him and picked up his drink in their stead.

There was never any glass of whiskey waiting for Penelope when she got home. Her lips curved up unbidden as she imagined her father's face, or Wiley's, if she asked for one, and ducked her head to hide the smile. God forbid a good little girl have a drink in the evenings. God forbid she ever relax, even in her own home. Instead, she was expected to perch daintily on the edge of the sofa, her hands folded neatly in her lap, listening expectantly to everything the men said—but never contributing.

"What do they want?" Ashes asked. He maintained the air of a benevolent leader, presiding over the small room, but Penelope knew he must have heard the rumors, same as anyone. The bank was as much a center of gossip as the post office and the general store.

Wiley shifted, his glance raking over the small pieces of paper in front of him. Penelope watched closely, wondering if his movement betrayed nerves she didn't see on his face. But he looked as relaxed as he ever did when she spied him through the window of the saloon, his boots propped up on the bar.

"The *Persephone Star* has been seen in the area," he said with relish, lingering on the name that caused so many others to quake.

Her father's thick gray eyebrows rose, not in surprise but in barely suppressed interest. "With or without Mirage Currier at the helm?"

Wiley sneered. "Seems that trumped-up little jilt is out of prison. I testified that she should be hanged, but the bottle-head of a federal marshal only managed to pin her sister for the murder. And she still hasn't swung yet."

An involuntary gasp escaped Penelope. "They're going to hang her sister?" It wasn't completely unheard of for a woman to hang, but it certainly wasn't common either. Penelope raised a hand to her throat, her fingers hovering uncertainly over the slender expanse of her neck. "But she's just a girl."

A cruel smirk twisted Wiley's lips. "'Just a girl'?" he parroted with delight. "From our own little postmistress?"

Penelope sank back against the cushions, away from the force of Wiley's unkind amusement. "I—" she began, but he held up a hand, hushing her.

"I told you," Wiley said, turning to her father. "These women activists want to play at being men when it suits them, but the second it doesn't, they hide behind their petticoats."

"I'm not an activist," Penelope said quickly. She read the news, she knew about the women fighting for suffrage. She read the accounts of the Seneca Falls Convention with bated breaths as a young girl, the incendiary words lighting up something inside her. But those revolutionary words hadn't actually started a revolution. Women still didn't have the vote. "I just like to feel useful."

"You'll feel useful soon enough," Wiley said, softening his tone. "When there are young ones to take up all the time you waste on your job and your little library."

Penelope dropped her eyes. "It's not a waste," she muttered, twining her fingers tightly in her lap. "Reading is important."

"Sure it is, peaches," Ashes said benevolently. "And you'll do plenty of reading to my grandbabies."

Penelope bit her lip. Babies and housekeeping were the only things Wiley or her father seemed to talk to her about these days. She remembered when she was younger; her father had talked to her about business. In each new town, he'd tell her the competition to his bank, the people resisting, and ask her to figure out how he should go about taking over the finances of the place. He'd smile proudly every time she got the answer right, telling her she was nearly as good at business strategy as he was.

He didn't talk to her about those things now. Not since she'd grown up, growing into a woman's body. He'd stopped including her then, stopped acting like it was the two of them against the world. Instead he sent for tutors and governesses, trying to train Penelope into being a "proper" woman.

Ashes had been thrilled when Wiley had come to him a few weeks before, sheriff's hat in hand, and asked for her hand in marriage. Now all he thought about was her ability to have babies.

Penelope swallowed down her retort, the words burning at the back of her throat. The library mattered to her, but it didn't matter to her father or to the man she was going to marry.

"What I want to know is what's taking them so long?" Ashes demanded. "That girl was convicted a year ago! Back in my day, a bandit would have been in the noose before the ink was dry on the execution order."

Wiley's lip curled up in a sneer. "They got them some sort of fancy New York lawyer. Been bombardin' the judge with bullshit appeals since the day they sentenced her. 'She's just a girl,'" he parroted, slanting an unpleasant glance at Penelope, who shrank back. "'She's just a child.' 'Not enough witnesses.' Codswallop like that. They still have one in the works, far as I know. Currier must know it'll be rejected, or she wouldn't be chasin' after me."

"And what are you going to do about her?" Ashes asked.

Wiley shrugged dismissively. "If Currier wants revenge, she knows where to find me." He took a slow, deliberate sip of his whiskey. "I ain't scared of no girl."

"Course not," Ashes agreed. "Bunch of girls running around playing at bandits. Maybe this time you'll get to put them all away for good."

"Get them all put in the ground, more like," Wiley said with a deep chuckle. To Penelope's horror, Ashes laughed along with him.

Penelope jerked up from her seat. "I'll just go check on Sarah and dinner," she said.

Ashes smiled encouragingly at her. "That's my good girl."

Penelope hurried out of the room before she had to hear anything further. She never felt more like an East Coast girl than when people talked about gunfights, bandits, and hangings. She knew Wiley thought she was uptight, but sometimes the Wild West was *too* wild for her. She didn't believe in the death penalty, and she certainly didn't believe that criminals should just be gunned down in the streets. The law said that people like Currier couldn't rob and steal, but it also said that she was owed a fair trial with an impartial judge. And Wiley was no impartial judge. If Currier came to Fortuna, there would be blood in the streets, and yet nobody seemed willing to do anything to stop it.

As Wiley took his leave at the end of the evening, he leaned in close to Penelope. For a moment, she thought he was going to kiss her, and barely managed to keep from drawing back. But instead he pushed his angry face close to hers and pointed a stern finger in her face. Fear swooped in Penelope's gut.

"You write back to that yellow-bellied sheriff over in Copper Creek and you tell him that as long as the *Persephone Star* is in *his* town, Currier is *his* problem. If he knows what's good for him, he'll arrest her, before he finds himself dealing with me."

Seeing he expected an answer, Penelope let out a shaky "All right."

Wiley stepped back, satisfied, and Penelope could breathe again. He tipped his hat up, staring down his nose at her. "Good girl," he said, before sauntering out the door. Penelope's stomach turned.

No crime has been committed in Copper Creek, and as long as it stays that way, Currier is free to do as she pleases.

Penelope looked down at the message in dismay. She had worded Wiley's threats and taunts as politely as she could, but it hadn't made any difference. The sheriff of Copper Creek wasn't going to act.

And she had to tell Wiley.

She'd worry herself sick about his reaction if she waited until evening to give him the message, so she locked up the post office and went straight to the sheriff's station.

Wiley was alone when she arrived. "What are you doing here?" he asked irritably.

Penelope tried not to take it personally. Wordlessly, she held out the telegram.

Wiley scanned it quickly and then dashed it to the desk with a thump of his fist. "I told you he was a coward."

"If she's committed no crime . . ." Penelope ventured.

"She's a criminal!" Wiley exploded.

Penelope staggered back from the force of his anger.

"That goddamn fool is going to get good men killed," Wiley ranted, shoving his chair back with a screech and lurching to his feet. "He's a lily-livered coward who deserves to be drawn and quartered for this. He should be charged with conspiring with criminals." He paced the room, muttering more to himself than Penelope. She frowned at the strength of his words, realization dawning upon her. Actions, crimes sent people to prison, not identities. Wiley couldn't lock Currier up just because she was a criminal, not when the justice system had let her out. But justice wasn't what Wiley was looking for.

"Am I the only real man in this goddamn territory?" Wiley demanded, wheeling on her. Penelope's eyes widened. "Am I the only one willing to deal with this situation the way it needs to be dealt with?" He thumped his revolver down on the desk with a resounding *clang*.

"I—I don't—"

"Well, that's fine," he snarled, ignoring her. "If no one else wants this fight, I'm happy to take it. Unlike those other milksops, I ain't got no problem showing that little girl what a *real* man is like." A nasty smile curled his lips. "You write back to that sniveling cur and you tell him that his townsfolk are lucky there's a real man within riding distance to do his job for him. You tell him I don't need him, because I got all I need right here." He patted the gun and Penelope gulped.

"I'll . . . write back," she promised halfheartedly.

Wiley smiled her out of the station. "You do that."

Outside, Penelope leaned against the wall and tried to steady her nerves. She thought the sheriff of Copper Creek had the right idea, staving off violence until it was an absolute necessity. But it was no surprise that Wiley didn't agree. He wasn't just *willing* to take on Currier; he *wanted* the fight. Penelope could tell he was practically salivating for it. But why?

It seemed Mirage Currier and the *Persephone Star* were all Fortuna could talk about. Messages continued to pour into the post office, and rumors sailed past on the wind.

"I hear she's a maniac—escaped from an asylum back east. She shoots people thinking they're demons."

"I hear she went to Boston to buy a gun more powerful than anything we've got out here, one that can blast a man at a hundred paces and keep firing for hours."

"I hear she didn't get it in Boston. She flew all the way to Europe to buy what they're using to fight the French."

"My husband says she's killed more people than you've laid eyes on in your life. Hundreds."

"No, thousands. And she's maimed more. She could fill up a hospital with how many people she's left bleedin' behind her."

"My cousin in Colorado said she's stolen millions of dollars. More money than any bank out here's got. She hides it in the boards of her ship. It's made of the stuff."

"Well, I heard from someone who knows that she's part Injun. Her mother was a Hopi, and she taught Mirage black spirit magic. She can kill a person just by looking at them."

"She conjures them spirit animals—bears and eagles that can rip a person through and then just *disappear*."

They burst through the tranquil bubble of the post office, a barrage of voices and rumors day in and day out. People trooped in with no business there at all, just to talk and talk and talk.

The people of Fortuna thought Penelope had inside information because she was the sheriff's fiancée, but Penelope felt more in the dark than anyone. She hadn't been in the territory during the *Persephone Star*'s reign of terror. She hadn't been in town when everyone slept with a pistol under their pillow and their money tight in hand.

She didn't even know what Currier looked like. The bandit could walk right by Penelope on the street, and she'd never know. She pictured the villains from the novels she read before bed: dark men with pointed beards and sinister eyes, heavy black cloaks and mysterious jagged scars. Brutish hands and teeth sharpened to vicious points.

It was hard to reconcile those images with the idea of a woman.

Of course, Penelope knew better than anyone that not all women were made the same—they weren't all soft, or feminine, or content to do nothing but raise babies.

Still, the more people talked, the more her nerves began to sing. Fear was a contagious disease, and the townspeople had been breathing it on her all day. No matter how wild the rumors, the core of what people were saying remained the same. Currier was coming for Sheriff Wiley and the town of Fortuna.

Penelope stepped into the general store, a hive of buzzing voices fanning the flames of fear higher and higher.

"I've been sleeping with my shotgun in my hand and my children in the bed," Elizabeth Mycock said, leaning insistently over the counter.

"What does Mirage Currier want with your children?" Marshal Amis scoffed from behind the flour.

"I'm protecting them!" Elizabeth said, scandalized.

"If you had a husband at home, instead of in the saloon, you wouldn't need to," Marshal muttered.

"Men don't understand the maternal spirit," Cathryn Houser sniffed, stepping up beside Elizabeth. "Two pounds of sugar, please," she said to the girl behind the counter.

Penelope slipped further into the store, trying to avoid catching the women's attention. The general store was always the center of the town activity; you could reckon on seeing at least half your neighbors every time you stepped inside.

"I remember the last time she was in the territory," Cathryn continued with a sigh. "I feel like we all aged a decade just knowing she was near."

"Ah, she ain't no different than any other bandit," Marshal insisted, pointing the spade he was examining at the two women. "We see murderers and bank robbers every day out here. It's why them city folks from the east can't hack it in the territories."

"Oh, really?" Elizabeth rolled her eyes. "If Currier came charging into your house demanding all your money, you'd stand up to her?"

"Damn right. Like any man would." Marshal drew himself up to his full height, his sunken chest proudly puffed. He was over seventy, his lined face in a perpetual frown.

"I'd like to see it," Cathryn snorted. "Oh! Penelope!"

Penelope slunk out from behind the wall of children's sweets. "Hello, Cathryn."

"I don't suppose you've heard?"

"Hmm?" Penelope reached out to inspect some checked muslin, feeling the fabric between her fingers.

"About Mirage Currier?"

She gave them her best blank look, one she had tested at length on Wiley and her father.

"Don't bother the poor girl," Elizabeth hissed. "She must be out of her mind with worry. If it was my John, I don't know what I'd do."

Marshal snorted ungraciously from the wall of seeds.

"Oh, she don't have to worry," Cathryn said wisely. "Sheriff Barnett can handle anything." She gave a sigh more befitting a schoolgirl than a woman of her age.

"I'll take some potatoes and flour," Penelope said to the girl behind the counter. Her eyes strayed out the window and over the horizon, toward Copper Creek. The town was thirty miles north, over four hours on horseback. But the *Persephone Star* was much faster.

Penelope had seen the airships back east, moving steadily through the skies, their ponderous bulk casting shadows on the buildings below. Not many made it out west, but small ones bought on the black market had become the transport of choice for a certain kind of criminal—ones who imagined themselves to be pirates of the skies, built on the old model.

She didn't doubt that Currier could have her ship in the air over Fortuna in an hour. And when she did raise anchor and sail their way, Penelope would be the first to hear about it. She would make sure that no matter what else happened, the sheriff of Copper Creek kept his eyes on the *Star*, and sent word the second the ship so much as drifted in the sky.

"Wiley knows what he's doing," she said mildly to the women. "It's why you all elected him sheriff, after all."

"Oh, of course he does," Elizabeth said quickly. "He's the best sheriff we ever had. And so handsome too." She tipped a secretive smile at Penelope.

Penelope accepted her purchases without sparing a glance at Elizabeth.

"I'll be seeing you all later," she said, forcing a smile.

"You tell Sheriff Barnett we all support him!" Cathryn called after her earnestly as Penelope hurried out the door.

"I told you," Wiley said that evening after dinner, a boastful grin on his face, "Currier's not man enough to face me." He laughed uproariously at his own joke.

The airship hadn't moved since it first came to anchor in Copper Creek. For all the rumors, for all the townspeople's certainty that

Currier was after Wiley, the outlaw didn't seem to be in a hurry to face Wiley gun-to-gun.

Penelope thought about the novels she read. "What if she's just waiting for you to let your guard down?" A smart outlaw wouldn't come charging in, guns blazing, not when she knew Wiley was waiting for her.

Wiley abruptly stopped laughing. "I'm the sheriff. My guard is never down."

Penelope faltered under his sharp gaze. "I didn't mean . . ."

"That I was neglecting my post?"

"No! I would never say that. You're an excellent sheriff." A wife was always loyal.

"Damn straight, I am," he said gruffly, but his temper cooled. "Best in all the territories. Quickest draw, too."

"Could hit a black cat in the dead of night," Ashes agreed jovially. Her father was unruffled as always—unless it was his money on the line.

"Still," Penelope said, biting her lip. She knew from the look on Wiley's face that she should keep her mouth shut—let the men talk about men's business, as they often reminded her—but Fortuna was her home too. People would get *hurt* if Wiley let the *Star* bring the fight to him. Law and order shouldn't mean gunfights in the street. "Don't you think you should call the federal marshal? Surely this is part of his job?"

"It's part of *my* job," Wiley said fiercely. "And I don't appreciate my own woman doubting I can do it."

"I didn't mean that," she said, dropping her eyes to the needlework in her lap. It was a mess; her hands weren't made for the quick, dexterous work on the best of days, and that night her thoughts were far too scattered for neat, even stitches. Yet another way in which she was an embarrassment to her sex. "I've just heard a lot of rumors about Currier. They say she's got an arsenal and she's coming for you personally. I . . ." Penelope stumbled over the words, searching for the right ones to quell the anger on Wiley's face. "I wouldn't want you to get hurt."

Her father's face softened, and he gestured between Penelope and Wiley with his whiskey glass. "Hear that? A woman has a right to worry," he soothed. Wiley slumped back in his chair, a lazy sprawl that disavowed her concern. But at least he didn't seem angry anymore.

"And maybe the girl's got a point," Ashes continued.

"I'll forgive a woman for not understanding the business of being a sheriff," Wiley said sharply. "But don't tell me you don't think I can handle some broad with a pistol."

"Now, now. You know I didn't mean that. But even a girl is liable to hit something if she gets off enough shots."

"Not if I get her right between the eyes, first," Wiley challenged.

Penelope frowned over her embroidery. They were talking about killing in cold blood as easily as if they were arguing over the price of whiskey down at the saloon. A point of pride and nothing more.

"That's assuming she plays fair, comes at you like a man in the street. But there's nothing right or honorable about a woman who takes to crime. Wench is likely to shoot you in the back."

"And it's not just Currier," Penelope said quietly. "She's got a whole crew."

"I got Lewis."

"Now, son, you and I both know Lewis Greenman isn't worth more than the leather his boots are made of," Ashes said.

Wiley had taken on the appearance of a cornered animal, and Penelope braced herself for the spitting hiss that might follow. He was as likely to storm out as listen seriously to their concerns. As Wiley often reminded her, a man didn't get to where he was without being a little reckless. For all she knew, he'd march himself straight to Copper Creek and get himself killed.

Wiley slammed his drink down on the table. "You think I need back up?"

"Now, Wiley, the girl's just looking out for her sweetheart. Think where you'd leave her if something happened to you."

Wiley regarded her for a long moment before saying tightly, "You're right. I wouldn't want you to worry."

She tried out a soft smile, the kind she saw women give their sweethearts. She imagined what she'd feel if Wiley died.

Sad. Of course she'd feel sad. Heartbroken. Probably.

The only problem was that Penelope didn't think she was in love with Wiley. Of course, she wouldn't have been before the proposal.

She barely knew the man. She knew *of* him, not just because the town was small enough that she knew everyone, but because as the sheriff he was, in some ways, the face of the town.

She hadn't done more than nod to him when he tipped his hat at her, though. He'd say hello in the store, or when he came into the post office. He'd smirk at her from the porch of the saloon with the rest of the men, but that wasn't anything about Penelope. They smirked at all the young women walking past.

Then one day she came home from work and found the sheriff sitting with her father in the parlor, big smiles on both of their faces. Good news, her father had said. And that was that. She was engaged.

He had admired her around town, or so he'd said. She was a decent, God-fearing woman, the kind the sheriff should marry. She was beautiful, he told her later, when Ashes let her see him out of the house, standing alone for five minutes in the dim light of the porch.

That had been flattering. Moving from town to town in the wake of her father's business, there hadn't been much time for men to come courting.

Plenty of the women around town told Penelope that love would come later. After the wedding. After the wedding night, and the babies that followed.

She'd get to know him then, in their house, and between their sheets.

But that wasn't the way love worked in the novels she read. The very idea of "getting to know" a man in that way, revealing herself before she even knew who he was, made her skin crawl.

Still, she softened her face, her lips curling in what she hoped was an approximation of love.

"I'll ask around town," Wiley relented, the fire in his eyes cooling at Penelope's smile. She must have been doing it right. "I'll deputize some more men, make sure they have my back when Currier comes to town."

"There." Ashes turned a broad grin on his daughter. "Now you can sleep and not be worryin' about your mister."

Penelope ducked her head over her work. With more men than just the scrawny nervous deputy at Wiley's back, he wouldn't be so quick to shoot, to kill. With numbers on his side, he could arrest

Currier and her crew peacefully, and make sure they got a fair trial. He could actually see that justice was served.

"Thank you," she told him and tried to bask in the smile he bestowed on her in return.

As the evening drew to a close, her father blinking blearily under the weight of his whiskey, Wiley stood, stretching to his full height. Penelope tucked her embroidery away more neatly than the work itself, and stood as well.

"Don't be out there too long," Ashes said, but his smile was teasing. Penelope tried to return it.

She walked Wiley to the door every night he dined with them. It was the only time they had ever spent alone, a few minutes standing in the dark of the porch. As alone as they could be with her father just inside and Sarah's voice warbling out through the open window, an off-tune rendition of the latest music hall favorite.

It wasn't a situation made for whispered sweet nothings, or frank discussions of the future—or their pasts. Mostly they stood in awkward silence until Wiley tipped his hat and sauntered off down the road.

Sometimes he stole a kiss. Or claimed one. Could it be called stealing when all her kisses were his due, for the rest of her life?

Tonight Wiley shoved his hands into his pockets and tipped his face up to the sky. The moon was near full and so bright it almost hurt to look at, lighting up the wispy clouds that smeared across the sky. It cast Wiley's face in dramatic relief, the silhouette of his nose, the sharp angles of his cheeks, the swath of his forehead shining silver while the heavy lines of his mouth retreated into shadows around his dark moustache. It made him look like a face on a coin, carved in profile to commemorate great deeds.

Penelope wondered if he did it on purpose, if he was thinking about his own life and the praise he might get for it.

"Sweet of you to fret about me," he said after a minute, voice low and gruff, the soft words odd coming from his mouth.

"Of course I do." It was automatic. She did sometimes think about his job, past the shiny badge on his chest and the honor of the first pew at church. It was dangerous; he put himself in harm's way on purpose to protect the town. She knew, intellectually, that Wiley could be hurt, or even killed, in his line of work.

But the whole of the West was dangerous. Bandits raided coaches on lonely roads, leaving the horses pulling into town with nothing but corpses dragged behind them. The ranchers on the outskirts of town were constantly clashing with the neighboring tribe over limited water, game, and land.

And when nobody was shooting guns, disease came and wiped out the few people that were left.

People died in the West. Penelope told herself that was why she didn't particularly worry about Wiley. Everyone's lives were dangerous.

"You gonna stay up late, weepin' your eyes out when I'm out on the job?" he asked, and Penelope faltered. She could hear that he was teasing, but her brain stuttered over the image of herself alone in a house, or surrounded by babies, never doing anything but waiting for him to come home. On the nights when Wiley didn't join Penelope and her father for dinner, she knew he often stayed out late at the saloon, while Penelope was tucked up safely in her house by early evening. But surely things were meant to be different once they were married?

"You won't stay out all night carousing when I'm waiting for you at home, will you?" she countered after a moment, hoping she matched his tone, hoping he didn't hear her pause.

"A man has a need for freedom," he said sternly. "I don't need no woman pinning me down."

What was the point of getting married, then? Penelope wondered despondently. *She'd* be pinned down, sure as the sun rose in the east.

"But when I've got a pretty little thing like you warming my bed, I might not have reason to be at the saloon all night," Wiley continued, stepping closer, a sly smile curving his lips. Women like Penelope weren't supposed to know about what happened behind the closed door of the saloon, but it wasn't like she could miss the young women who lived above the bar, smoking cigars out the window in low-cut dresses, their drunken raucous laughter carrying through the streets. She knew whoring was considered normal for a man like Wiley, but it made her stomach turn.

Wiley brushed a lock of curly hair away from her face, tucking it behind her ear and then keeping his hand there, trailing down the length of her slender neck. The touch was light enough to make her shiver in the oppressive heat of the night. It didn't last for long. His hand curved over her, gentleness falling away, grip tight around the back of her neck.

She froze, locked in place.

"You lookin' forward to the wedding night?" he asked. His tone was lewd, even if his words were not. For one brief moment, she felt like she could see everything he wanted to do to her burning in the depths of his dark, hot eyes.

She dropped her gaze, stammering, humiliation welling up to press behind her eyes, stinging.

A gentleman wasn't supposed to talk like that, for all he was her fiancé. The men in her books never did.

"Look at that pretty blush." The words rumbled out so low he might have been speaking them to himself. His fingers tightened on her neck, and Penelope gasped as he dragged her in, pulling her against the hard line of his body. He crushed his mouth down upon hers, his moustache prickling her face as his lips pried her mouth open.

His tongue pushed inside, an aggressive, wet slide. She shuddered, caught in his grip like a bug pinned to a board. Her arms hung limply at her sides and she squeezed her eyes shut, hoping it would end.

Wiley's other arm snaked around Penelope's waist, jerking her closer, bowing her back painfully under the squeeze of her corset.

He delved into her mouth for a long moment, until her jaw ached and her face burned.

Finally he let go, pushing her back enough to make her stumble. He smirked as she struggled to right herself, smoothing her skirt, her hair, hands flying over herself nervously, as if she expected to find a part of herself missing.

"Night, sweetheart." He tipped his hat in a crude imitation of courtesy and sauntered off the porch.

Penelope gripped the railing and squeezed her eyes shut, taking a steadying breath.

She could feel the scrape he'd left across her face and lips. She cupped a hand over her mouth, hiding the evidence, and let herself back into the quiet house.

 # III.

Wiley prowled the town like a mountain lion, fierce and hungry. He stalked down Main Street, his shoulders tight with anger and his fists bunched at his side. The most hardened men, the ranchers from the surrounding desert who'd shoot a man before they'd tip their hat at him, jumped out of his way, ducking into the barbershop to watch him storm past.

Penelope saw him through the window of the post office, the line of her counter underscoring his anger as he stalked by. She ducked her head over the telegraph and willed him to keep walking.

When Charlotte Storey slipped in twenty minutes later, there was something like pity in her eyes.

Penelope bit her lip. Had Wiley told the menfolk about their kiss the night before, painting her as a fast woman? Shame twisted ugly and deep in her chest whenever she thought about it. Not only that it had happened, but that she was supposed to enjoy it. That she might have a lifetime of kisses like that ahead of her.

"You must be real worried, honey," Charlotte said, leaning over the counter.

"Worried?"

"About those terrible outlaws," Charlotte said, eyes wide. "Threatening the sheriff."

"Oh, yes," Penelope said weakly. "Of course I am."

"I just can't imagine what I'd do if it was my husband facing something like that. I think I'd make him leave town!"

"Wiley would never abandon Fortuna." Penelope said mechanically. Or, at least, he wouldn't back down from a fight.

"No, of course not." Admiration shone in Charlotte's watery blue eyes. "That's why he's the sheriff. I just wish some of the men were brave enough to stand up with him. It's a crying shame to leave him facing those she-devils all alone."

"What do you mean?"

"Haven't you heard?" Charlotte leaned closer, gossip gleaming in her eyes. "Why, your man's been up and down this town ten times today, trying to gather up a posse to face the Currier gang."

"Yes," Penelope said slowly. "He wanted— I mean, *I* wanted him to have backup."

"Of course you do," Charlotte nodded. "But everyone's said no." She shook her head sagaciously. "I can't believe this town is so full of cowards. My Bill would have been with the sheriff in an instant, only he hurt his back last year tilling our crops."

No wonder Wiley had looked so angry. Forced to ask for help only to find out no one would stand with him. Penelope softened, feeling sorry for the man. "I should go and see him," she decided.

"Oh, of course," Charlotte smiled. "I remember what it was like to have a sweetheart, back when Bill and I were young."

Charlotte was no older than Penelope, but she'd been married since she was seventeen. A fact she liked to dangle in Penelope's face from time to time.

Penelope organized her papers and reached for the large ring of keys she kept by the desk. "You didn't have anything urgent, did you Charlotte?"

"Oh no. I just wanted to check that you were all right."

Penelope forced a tight smile onto her lips. Ushering the woman out of the office, she locked the door behind her and turned her steps resolutely toward the sheriff's office. It was her duty, after all, to look after the emotional well-being of her fiancé. She had a lifetime of appeasing him in her future.

Wiley was seated when Penelope walked in, his muddy boots up on his desk and his hat tipped forward over his face. He was laughing. "Hey, darlin'. What are you doing here?"

Penelope lingered just inside the doorway, her eyes darting around the station. Lewis Greenman, the timid deputy, hovered nervously by the back door, fidgeting with some papers. Another man sat in the corner, and she blinked against the dimness of the office for a second before she recognized the face of Mace Toluth, one of the barmen from the saloon. He had a bottle of booze at his lips.

"Oh." She shifted nervously. The scene wasn't at all what she had expected to find. She thought there would be feathers to soothe, but it seemed Wiley had skipped right to getting drunk. "I thought I'd stop by and see how you were."

"We're fine, aren't we, Mace?" Wiley tipped a wink at the other man. Lewis frowned.

"I, um..." Penelope faltered. She knew better than to make Wiley look weak in front of another man. "I heard you were getting your posse together," she said diplomatically.

"Sure am."

"And you're not having any problems?" She looked desperately over to the frowning deputy. "Lewis?"

The deputy's eyes widened. "N-no. Of course not," he faltered, then blanched. "I mean, there were *some* problems, but not really *problems*, if you see what I'm saying, Miss Moser."

"Why?" Wiley swung his feet to the floor and sat forward, cutting off Lewis's fumbling words. "You hearin' rumors about what a lot of yelpers this town is made up of?" A slow smirk replaced the disdain on his face. "Don't go worryin' your little head about it. I got all the real men I need to face those sinnin' molls."

"Oh." Penelope's gaze snuck back to Mace. He was a big fellow, and meaner sober than he was drunk, which was saying something.

"Yeah, Mace here's going to help me out. And Platt Dempsey, Moody Alberts, and good ol' Seth Byrne. Fellas not afraid to stand up for what's right."

Penelope's heart sunk. Wiley had rattled off the names of the cruelest, roughest, drunkest louts Fortuna had to offer.

Penelope held her tongue until the evening. She certainly couldn't object in front of Mace, or even her father, and so she waited anxiously by her front door, peering through the sidelights for a glimpse of Wiley's figure on the road. She had hoped that by finding help, Wiley would prevent a massacre, but instead he had practically guaranteed one. She couldn't be the only one that saw that people, *innocent* bystanders, would get hurt.

Finally, a tall figure crested the horizon of the street, his boots kicking up red dust in his wake. Penelope eased open the front door and slipped out onto the porch, trying not to draw the attention of the rest of the house.

If anyone saw her slip out, they would probably think she was meeting Wiley for a kiss before dinner.

She frowned, bracing herself on the smooth wooden railing of the porch as she awaited his approach. Wiley spotted her from down the lane and tipped his hat.

"You've been spending an awful lot of your day lookin' out for me, darlin'," he drawled when he was in earshot. "Finally excited for this marriage business?"

Penelope fought the blush that threatened to engulf her cheeks at Wiley's words. "I wanted to speak to you before dinner."

He mounted the porch steps in a slow swagger. "All right."

Penelope had spent the day choosing her words carefully. "I'm worried about you in this fight with Mirage Currier."

An exasperated sound slipped past Wiley's lips. "I did what you asked. I got my posse. We can handle a couple of girls playin' at being men."

The words nettled. Either Currier's gang was a bunch of little girls or they were hardened criminals who deserved to hang. They couldn't be both.

"Of course," Penelope soothed. "But the men you chose. They're not the most reliable."

"I've known Mace and Seth since I got to Fortuna. And Platt Dempsey ran the gold rush with Mace. He vouches for him."

As if Mace's word meant anything. The only thing you could trust when it came to Mace was that he always had at least one more trick up his sleeve.

"Moody Alberts is a drunk," Penelope said bluntly, latching on to the one man Wiley wasn't defending. "How do you know he'll even show up when Currier comes to town?"

"He used to have a wife," Wiley said, smiling nastily. "Ran off with one of the saloon girls in Socatoon, and not for the drinks she was servin'. He's got a bullet ready for every whore who thinks they can replace a man between some broad's legs."

They were words no gentleman should ever say to a lady, and Penelope couldn't help the way she gasped.

Wiley barked out a laugh. "Don't get your underthings in a twist. I'm just tellin' you how it is."

Penelope wondered if he was right. He'd been dropping a lot of hints about how "unnatural" and "sinful" Currier and her gang were, but this was the first time he'd come right out and said it: women lying with other women like they were men.

Penelope knew she should be horrified, but instead she was curious. It was something that had never come up in any of her books. She didn't even know how it worked. She knew what she had between her legs, and had a vague idea of what lay between Wiley's. She'd seen enough dogs mating in the streets to know how parts locked together and babies were made. It didn't look pleasant, but she understood the biology of it. But she couldn't imagine how what she had beneath her petticoats would fit with another woman's.

She shook her head resolutely. "I know some of those men are your friends, but you've also arrested each of them a dozen times. Seth Byrne spends more time in your jail cell than his own home!"

Wiley shrugged easily. "He gets a little out of hand when he drinks, and so I bring him in to cool down. He don't have a wife to report to, so who cares if he spends some time in the saloon?"

It was more than "some time" and Wiley knew it. Seth Byrne had never done an honorable day's work in his life. He'd come out west to make his fortune, but realized it took just as much hard work in the territories as it had back in Boston. Since then he'd been picking up odd jobs and losing them as soon as he could change the money for whiskey.

"Platt Dempsey beats his wife, and Moody and Seth spend half their lives dead drunk in the middle of town. Mace has been in more fights than a professional boxer."

"Hey," Wiley snapped. "Don't go badmouthin' my pals."

"I just don't see how they're supposed to diffuse the situation!"

"'Diffuse the situation,'" Wiley parroted. "Jesus. You plannin' on runnin' for mayor or something? Here in Fortuna we take care of our problems. And I've picked the best men in town to do that."

Anger bubbled up inside Penelope. "The best men in town turned you down. What you've got now are a bunch of lowlifes and criminals who want an excuse to shoot at someone."

Rage passed like a dark cloud over Wiley's face, and Penelope knew she'd gone too far. She took a few hesitant steps back.

"Don't go defendin' those yellow bastards who wouldn't stand up for this town. My men are the only ones willing to put themselves in harm's way to keep you and yours safe, so think better of it before you go mouthin' off."

"I'm not," Penelope said quickly. She took a deep, steadying breath. "But, Wiley, they only want bloodshed. It'll turn into a showdown."

"So?" The anger had drained from Wiley's face, replaced with brash defiance.

"So?" Penelope said shrilly. "How is that supposed to keep anyone safe?"

"My guys know their way around a gun," he said, digging his heels in, stubborn as a mule. "It's only the criminals who are in danger. Unless it's them you're worried about?" He arched a challenging eyebrow.

Penelope raised her chin defiantly. "They don't deserve to die." She believed that with all her heart and soul. She wasn't going to take the words back, no matter how fierce Wiley looked.

But Wiley laughed. "Don't they? One of them's already on the gallows for what they did. I think the rest of them should follow her right down to hell."

He spat the words, and Penelope's grip on the railing tightened in shock.

"They haven't even done anything yet!" she protested.

"They did more than enough before."

"Not enough to still be in prison."

"Hey," Wiley said, voice sharp as a bullet cracking through the air. "*I'm* justice in this town. Me. I decide who deserves what's coming to them."

It wasn't right. "That's not how the law works," she argued, surprised at her own gumption. "Back east—"

"This ain't back east," Wiley interrupted with a sneer. "With your drawing rooms, and your evening salons, and your men in brocade and polished shoes. This here is the territories."

"There are still laws," Penelope said, voice shaking.

"Yeah. Me," Wiley snarled. "Judge, jury, and executioner."

"What did Currier do that she deserves to die in the streets?" she demanded. "Tell me. Tell me what makes her such a monster."

Wiley clenched his jaw, but Penelope rushed on. "I wasn't there. I don't know what happened. I don't even know what her sister's hanging for!"

Wiley took a conciliatory step back. "They're criminals." His voice was carefully even. "Outlaws. Bandits. Murderers. They deserve everything that's coming to them."

"Then why won't you tell me what actually happened when they were in the territory last?"

"They broke the law. I arrested them. They went to jail. What more do you need to know?" He narrowed his eyes slyly at her. "You one of those women who gets all hot and bothered hearing 'bout guns and killin'?"

"What? No!"

"You want me to whisper to you what it feels like to watch someone die?"

Penelope shook her head, a curl slipping loose from the knot on the back of her head, falling into her eyes. "No. You know that's not what I meant."

"Then maybe you should just keep out of things that aren't your business."

He turned his back on her sharply, yanking the door open and letting himself into the house. She watched him go, hearing the echo of his heavy boots down the hall. She was certain now. Wiley was going to kill every last crewmember of the *Persephone Star*, and she had no idea why.

 # IV.

It had been seven days since word of the *Persephone Star* first came to Fortuna. But anyone who hoped the threat would blow over would be holding their breath for a while longer. Penelope looked down at the latest message from Copper Creek and her stomach turned.

Natives had come to the outskirts of town, horses pulling a wagon overflowing with weapons. Not native weapons, either. Army guns and munitions. Fancy things that could shoot more bullets in a minute than a man could dream of.

Everyone could guess where the tribe had gotten them, pulled off the bodies they felled as the Army pushed farther and farther into land that didn't belong to them. Trying to steal the natives' land and freedom, and losing their own lives in the process.

Bandits stole from tribal lands just as readily as from the established towns. They raided whatever they could get their hands on and weren't too high and mighty for native food and supplies.

But in this case it looked like it was true that "my enemy's enemy is my friend." Whether Currier was really part Hopi, or she had an understanding with the natives, or they just wanted to watch the white men burn, the natives came to Copper Creek and sold every last weapon to the *Persephone Star*.

Currier's gang was ready for a battle, and Penelope didn't see any way to keep war from coming to Fortuna.

She thought about the hard line of Wiley's mouth when he dismissed her questions, waving off her concerns before dinner, during dinner, and in their awkward good night. He told her she was just a woman, that she wouldn't understand.

Yet it was a woman he was saddling up to kill, a woman who was arming herself to the teeth and coming for his neck.

She knew Wiley had locked up the whole crew a year before, and she knew that Currier's sister was still in prison, readying to hang.

That was *all* she knew, though. It was driving her mad. There wasn't a single bit of town business or local gossip that Penelope didn't know inside and out. Every piece of good news or bad came through the line and through her hands before it ever found its way to its intended recipient, but everything with Currier and her gang had happened before she came to town. It was old Mr. Gillespie manning the Line, and he had left town days after Penelope took over as postmistress. Everything he knew about the situation rode out of town on the late coach with him.

Whenever Currier was mentioned in town, everything was hushed whispers and significant looks. Nothing to give Penelope any idea why Currier was different from any of the other criminals Wiley had put away in his time as sheriff. She sank back in her chair and frowned out the window. She wondered what it would be like—not robbing and killing, but being on her own. Currier had her crew, of course, but they were women too. Currier was the boss. There was no one to answer to, no father, no husband, no children. Just Mirage and her ship and the open skies.

People in town hissed under their breath about how unnatural it all was, but Penelope didn't see why. Oh, she knew women should be quiet and modest, and go to church and take care of children. She'd heard it every day of her life. But she didn't see what made her so different from Wiley or any of the other men about town, who got to go where they liked, wear what they liked, and didn't have to answer to anyone but the law. Women were constantly being told how to dress, what to say, and how to think. Even in all of Penelope's novels, where women had opinions and voiced them to whomever would listen, they always ended up with a husband, quiet and subdued.

That was where she was going to end up too. So even though she knew Currier was a monster for murdering people, Penelope respected her too, for finding a way to be herself, outside the system that kept women like Penelope pinned.

She sighed, sending a message back to Copper Creek, reminding them of their promise to watch Currier every second of the day.

She tucked the telegram into the pocket of her heavy skirt and started packing up, casting a glance out the window at the sun, which was dipping over the horizon. Another late night in the office. She'd take the message straight to Wiley at the station and see if he was feeling any more reasonable than the night before.

The sun was still hot despite the settling dusk. Penelope fanned herself as she stepped out of the office, locking the door securely behind her. She smiled and nodded her way down the street, trying to pretend everything was all right.

The door of the sheriff's station was unlocked. Penelope squinted as she stepped over the threshold, looking for signs of Wiley. His chair was empty, the desk tidy enough except for the dirt his boots always left on the right-hand side. The small jail cell at the back stood empty, miraculously free of one of the local drunks sleeping off his liquor. Penelope shook her head and peered around the doorway to the back room. Weapons lined the largest wall of the small cupboard, fancy things with gleaming parts that Penelope didn't think she'd ever understand.

Wiley didn't seem to be there. The corners of Penelope's mouth dipped down as she hurried back into the main office, ducking her head to peer through the dusty window. Wiley could have been called out on a job, but it was just as likely he'd forgotten to lock up the office in his hurry to get a drink with the boys. On nights when he didn't join them for dinner, Wiley propped up the bar at the saloon, drinking until Mace finally threw them all out for the evening.

She turned away from the window as a faint upbeat tune from the saloon's automated piano caught on the breeze.

If men and women talked more, if they were open with each other, Penelope thought there wouldn't be so much need for whiskey and loose women.

If Wiley would talk to her about the Currier situation, instead of getting angry every time she brought it up . . . If he would just *tell* her what had happened that day . . .

Penelope narrowed her eyes thoughtfully as her gaze swept over the empty office. She had never been in the sheriff's station without Wiley or Lewis there. She took a hesitant step toward the door and then stopped. If anyone came in, she could say she was looking for her fiancé. There was nothing wrong with that. It was expected, even.

Penelope reached out and pushed the door shut, closing herself in the dark interior of the office.

Lewis kept all the station's files in the back room, stacked unceremoniously on the shelves across from the weapons store. Wiley was always telling him to get the papers in order or get rid of them, but Lewis wasn't the most efficient man on a good day.

Penelope left the electric lights off in the main office, grabbing a single candle from the stockroom and lighting it with shaky hands. She didn't know exactly what she was looking for, but she got an uneasy feeling in her stomach every time Wiley refused to answer her questions. Penelope hated not knowing. No matter the subject, if there was information to be had, she wanted it. It was why the New York library remained lodged in her heart. It was why she had answered the advertisement for a new postmaster when she moved to Fortuna.

The little town was full of secrets, and some of them might be in this crowded back room.

The papers weren't in anything resembling an order, but Lewis compulsively kept everything: logs of arrests, warrants, and every letter and telegram the office received. Penelope's own handwriting dotted the pile, her neat print covering the telegrams from the last nine months. She pushed them aside; she was looking for information from before she arrived in Fortuna. Hiking her skirts around herself, she dropped to her knees, quick hands darting into the stacks and moving papers aside.

Penelope worked rapidly, picking up each piece of paper and setting it aside, sorting them into piles like Lewis should have done years before. Most of it was useless or unintelligible. Code words and names littered every document, law enforcement speak for something that should have been straightforward and simple like *drunk and disorderly*. Finally, Penelope found a telegram in a messy scrawl, the shaky handwriting of Rodney Gillespie, the postmaster before her. He'd been eighty-two when he finally stepped down from the job, and it showed in the unevenness of his script. She squinted at the paper, trying to decipher his writing.

It turned out to be a message from Lewis's mother back in Kansas, telling him his pa was sick. Mr. Greenman had died nearly a year before, and Penelope tucked the telegram away with a twinge of guilt.

The next one she found had more to offer—it was the summons for Wiley to travel to White Hills and testify against the *Persephone Star* gang, dated July twenty-second.

Penelope started a new pile then. Anything related to the Currier case.

Further down in the mess, she discovered an old newspaper from White Hills—*Bloody Shoot-out Leaves Beloved Mayor Dead*. She sat back on her heels hard. There it was in black-and-white: murder. The weapons on the wall gleamed eerily in the candlelight, the brass and bronze catching the flame and reflecting it back at strange angles.

She scanned the article. It was mostly a memorial to the fallen mayor, detailing his civic improvements and his clean living. The outlaws were described as "maddened harlots" and the paper gloated over the arrests that had been made—five members of the gang. The article concluded: *The only eyewitness to the murder of Mayor Bailey, Sheriff Wiley Barnett, will testify against the criminals.*

Why hadn't Wiley told her? His anger made more sense now. She didn't believe in the death penalty, but she understood why people wanted it in cases like this. An eye for an eye. Based on the article, Mayor Bailey had been a good man. He tried to clean up the worst of White Hills, cracking down on the gambling and boozing that seemed to dominate every town in the territory. He had a wife and children young enough to feel his loss. She chewed her lip, gazing down at the picture of the murdered man.

Corinna Currier pulled the trigger, but Penelope could understand why Wiley blamed the whole gang. They caused the shoot-out, and the mayor wasn't the only one hurt. Penelope could imagine the same carnage happening on the main street of Fortuna, Cathryn Houser or Elizabeth Mycock running from a rain of bullets. She shuddered.

It was dark in the back room, and Penelope's father would be growing anxious about where she was. She tugged her watch from the pocket of her waistcoat and flipped open the lid, the light of the candle catching softly on the rose gold.

She could spare another quarter of an hour. Uneasiness still churned in her stomach. She just couldn't understand why Wiley was so cagey about this case, when the paper made it seem so clear-cut.

Decided, she began making her way through the pile more swiftly, trying to discard anything that wasn't immediately relevant.

There were more newspapers, all related to the Currier case. Headline after headline proclaiming stays of execution, each more hysterical than the last, chronicling the appeals in the case that had put Wiley in such a rage. *Dangerous Bandit Granted a Pardon?* one provocatively asked. Under the headline was a grainy photo. Corinna Currier stared out from the paper, eyes wide and lips tight. Penelope found it difficult to tear her gaze away from those frightened eyes. The girl looked like she was little more than a child, yet someone in the sheriff's office had taken a pen and doodled a noose around her slender neck in thick, black ink. Penelope was willing to guess who'd done it. With gentle hands, she set the paper aside, her eyes lingering over the image, so starkly contrasted with the headline that screamed Corinna's guilt.

Biting her lip, Penelope turned back to the rest of the files. An envelope sticking out of a sheath of newsprint caught her eye. Wiley's hasty penmanship was scrawled across the front, addressed to Deputy Greenman.

It was wrong to open another person's mail; as postmistress, that was at the heart of Penelope's moral compass. It was a federal offense. But this envelope had been opened long before; the seal was broken and the paper ripped. And she had to know.

She eased the letter out of its casing and held it close to the flame of her candle.

Lewis—

Get the 10 o'clock coach to W.H. You're testifying about the shooting tomorrow afternoon. Need you to back up my story.

WB

Penelope frowned over the paper. It was dated July twenty-fourth—two days after the telegram summoning Wiley. Wiley had taken the coach to White Hills just the day before; if Lewis was needed to be a witness, why hadn't the deputy been called along with his sheriff?

She glanced back over her shoulder at the newspaper she had stacked with the telegram. Reporters got stories wrong all the time, but the paper had said Wiley was the only witness to the shooting.

So what could Lewis say to back up his testimony?

She frowned at the letter thoughtfully. It was possible that Lewis was just called upon because he'd been at the fight. The judge would want to speak to everyone who had participated in the shoot-out and lived to talk about it. Still, she put the letter aside carefully.

Her gaze strayed back to the newspaper, wondering again if the reporter had simply gotten the story wrong. Her frown deepened. The date on the paper was July eighth. The shoot-out had happened the day before.

The date stuck in Penelope's mind, and she turned back to the pile of discarded paper. There, in Rodney Gillespie's shaky script, was a receipt for a telegram sent. She wrote out a dozen of the same little slips every day. But this one was for a telegram sent by Lewis Greenman, from Fortuna to his mother in Kansas, on July seventh—the day of the shooting in White Hills.

Penelope's eyes widened. Lewis Greenman hadn't been in White Hills at all. So what testimony could he possibly have given at the trial?

Penelope glanced at her watch again, groaning at the time. Her father would never believe she had been at the office, not at this late hour. She picked up the piles of papers hastily, mixing them back up in some semblance of the disorder she had found them in. But she hesitated over the telegram receipt and Wiley's letter. Something didn't add up between the letter, the receipt, and the newspaper, and Penelope was determined to find out what it was. She wondered if there was anything in her own beloved post office that might shed light on the situation. Postmaster Gillespie had been almost as much of a pack rat as Lewis Greenman. She determined to search the office the next day. After all, a girl was going to hang on the basis of whatever testimony Wiley and Lewis had given at trial. She didn't think anyone deserved it, murderer or no, but if anything untoward had happened at the trial? Well, she was going to get to the bottom of it.

Decided, she looked around the small room, taking in a stack of boxes that had a thick layer of dust covering them. Lewis surely wouldn't miss the papers, and if he did, well . . . they'd still be in the office, wouldn't they? She slipped the letter and the receipt into the narrow space between two boxes; she'd come back for them if they turned out to be important.

Penelope hurried out of the room, depositing the candle back in the storeroom and stepping through the darkened office and out onto the street.

Something coarse pulled roughly over her face, blocking out the light of the moon and muffling her scream. She heard a frantic curse, and then everything went dark.

V.

Penelope blinked, her vision swimming and her head aching. She immediately squeezed her eyes shut against the blinding light with a groan. She could hear voices nearby, and the hardness at her back told her she was lying on the floor.

Had she fainted in the post office?

Taking a deep breath, she cracked her eyes open again, regretting it instantly as her headache throbbed to the fore.

She definitely wasn't in the office.

Low beams, rough-hewn out of dark, aged wood, loomed over her head. Penelope's stomach turned as she rotated her head, queasiness rising up in the back of her throat at the motion. There were no windows in the small compartment she found herself in; the space was lit by electric lights. Barrels lined the walls, leaving barely enough room for Penelope.

Penelope struggled up to her elbows, frowning. Where was she?

It took a few minutes for her to sit fully upright, choking back the vomit that threatened to crawl up her throat. She clapped a hand over her mouth and whimpered. Her head throbbed viciously, and although she couldn't remember what had happened, she must have bumped it something fierce.

Once, when she was a small girl, she had taken her horse out for a joyride, slinging her legs on either side of the saddle with the thrill of the forbidden. She had galloped across the field adjacent to their homestead and let out a whoop at the feel of the wind in her hair and the horse's powerful muscles between her thighs. It was nothing like the sedate rides she took with her father, legs tucked to the side on a lady's saddle.

She hadn't seen the snake that slithered out across the path, sunning its scales in the afternoon heat, but her horse certainly had. He'd reared. She'd had the wind knocked right out of her, and she'd lain there on the path, stunned, as the horse galloped away.

She'd knocked her head on a rock when she fell, and her hair was gummy with drying blood. Her head had ached then too, a dull, insistent hurt that lasted hours and had the maids all tutting over her for the next few days.

Penelope's head hurt worse than that now, and she could recognize a bump to the skull when she felt one. She raised a shaky hand to the back of her head and, sure enough, found a goose egg rising up under the mass of her hair. Her fingers were clean when she pulled them away, though, and she sent up a prayer for small blessings.

What she couldn't understand was *how* she had come to bump her head. She wasn't a clumsy woman, and she hadn't been anywhere near a horse. The last thing she remembered was going to the sheriff's office looking for Wiley.

A noise of surprise slipped past her lips as the night came back to her through the fog of her headache, and she slumped against a barrel, wondering if she'd brought this upon herself by snooping.

Of course, she didn't know what *this* was, except for a fierce headache and a strange room.

It looked like a storage compartment or a pantry, except that the barrels looked nothing like the usual kegs of flour or sugar that the general store stocked. In fact, the closest thing Penelope had ever seen to them were the weekly deliveries to the saloon, large casks sloshing full of whiskey.

She gave the air a delicate sniff and her stomach turned again. There was the distinct scent of alcohol on the air. She sat up a little straighter at that. Was she in the saloon?

She knew Wiley had been out boozing while she searched his office—had he found her somehow? She hesitantly touched the back of her head again with her fingers. No, she wouldn't believe it of him. Wiley had a temper, but he wouldn't *hit* her outright. Not with the whole town watching their courtship.

So what on earth had happened?

Penelope crawled over to the door, her skirts bunching uncomfortably under her knees. She jiggled the heavy iron handle and wasn't surprised when it didn't give. Still, panic hummed in the back of her head, an insistent reminder that she didn't know where she was and she couldn't get out. The close walls of the small room seemed to creep even nearer.

Someone must have heard the jiggling of the handle, because before she could get too worked up, the door flew open.

"Well, look who's awake."

The woman in the doorway wore a black corset with nothing over top of it, the round globes of her breasts pushed to prominent notice. Her skirt, if it could be called that, was made of the kind of cheap stuff dance hall girls wore, and had been sheared off above the knee, offering glimpses of pale thigh. The expanse of her unstockinged legs was only broken by the high boots she wore.

Penelope averted her eyes, panic clutching at her. Somehow she had found herself in a brothel.

"Oh," the woman said, half under her breath. "Wait till the captain sees *you*."

That did not help with Penelope's panic. "I don't know how I got here," she said quickly, "but there's been a mistake. I'm a lady."

"You sayin' I ain't?" the woman asked, cocking a hip. The movement exposed more of her legs, and Penelope gulped.

"I'm pure," she whispered to the floor. "Please." She'd heard tales of women kidnapped and sold into prostitution, but she had never thought it could happen to her. "My father has money. He'll pay for my release."

"Is that so?" the woman asked, a twinkle in her eyes. "I'll be sure to pass that on to the captain. But as for your purity, I don't really give a rat's ass one way or the other. But since we're gossiping, I'm *not*." She tipped a saucy wink at Penelope.

Before Penelope could respond, the woman turned away. "Hey, Captain! This nice *lady* we got has finally woken up, and I think you better come talk to her, because she seems to think I got designs on her maidenhead."

The coarse language brought a blush to Penelope's cheeks.

"Well, do you?" another voice drawled. A petite figure sauntered into view. This woman was smaller than the first, but somehow seemed to take up all the space in the room as she ducked her head into the compartment to peer at Penelope.

Her appearance was no less shocking than the first woman's. She was wearing britches, and she had a holster strapped round her hips, a pistol and a dagger glinting in the light of the hall. Who *were* these women?

The britches were almost more obscene than the length of the first woman's skirt. The tight cut of them revealed the shape of the woman's body: ankles, calves, round thighs, and gently curving hips. Something about the soft lines of those curves brought heat to Penelope's cheeks. She gulped, surprised at her own reaction. She was blushing like a schoolgirl when a handsome man tipped his hat at her. But there were no men here.

Flustered, she dragged her gaze up away from the woman's body, but the sight that greeted her was no less surprising. The woman's dark hair was shorn off just below her ears. It made her look almost boyish despite her feminine curves—or maybe *impish* was the right word, as she smirked down at Penelope.

"So." She raised an eyebrow. "Who the hell are you?"

"What?" Penelope spluttered. That was the last question she'd been expecting. "Who are *you*?"

The woman struck a cocky pose. "Mell Currier. Pleasure to make your acquaintance."

"Currier?" Penelope's eyes widened, and she frantically tried to crabwalk away from the door. A barrel at her back stopped her. "*Mirage* Currier?"

A moue of displeasure crossed the woman's lips. "I said Mell, didn't I? Do I look like some illusion to you?"

"But you are— I mean, you're . . ." Penelope cut herself off, looking wildly around at the wood slatting of the walls and the heavy dark beams. "My God. This is the *Persephone Star*, isn't it?"

The smile returned to Mell's lips. "The one and only," she said, patting the ship's side fondly. "Now, it seems you know more than enough of who I am. So let's get back to my question: Who are you?"

"If you don't know who I am, what am I doing here?"

A million reasons for Mirage Currier to kidnap her had raced through Penelope's mind, from ransoming her to Ashes to holding her hostage to negotiate with Wiley. But she couldn't figure out why they'd take her if they didn't know her connection to the two most important men in Fortuna.

"Ah. About that," Mell said, looking embarrassed. "Got a girl in my crew. She's a great gal and the best shot in the West, but she don't always think things through. I sent her to surprise that damned weaselly sheriff of Fortuna, and somehow she came back with *you*. I can't explain how that happened, and neither can Ruth, so why don't you give it a try?"

"Surprise Wi—the sheriff?" Penelope repeated, ignoring Currier's question. "Do you mean *kidnap*?" The memory of a bag pulling down over her head came flooding back.

"What business I got with the sheriff is no business of yours," Mell said stubbornly. "But Ruth tells me *you* were coming out of the sheriff's office in the dark of the night. So what were you doing there? You some kind of lady robber?"

"What? Like you?"

"Hey now," Mell said with a cocky grin. "I ain't no lady."

"I can see that," Penelope muttered, her eyes straying to the tight fabric of Mell's trousers once again.

"So what business did you have in the sheriff's office after dark? You his mistress?"

"How dare you!" Penelope gasped.

"Nah, she's very insistent about the state of her maidenhead," the other woman drawled from the sidelines. "Pure as snow, she says she is."

Mell slanted an interested look at Penelope. "Did she?" she murmured.

"I *am*. Not that it's any of your business."

"Then why'd you tell me about it?" The woman crossed her arms over her chest, and a bit more of her breasts was exposed.

"I thought this was a brothel," Penelope hissed, embarrassed.

She expected them to be offended, but Mell just barked out a laugh. "I guess I can see where you'd get that impression, but Vera's no whore. Not anymore."

There was a protective fondness in Mell's tone that surprised Penelope. Vera's former career was less of a surprise, given the state of her clothes.

No wonder the good townsfolk were always talking about Currier's crew as a bunch of sinners.

Not that Penelope thought it was the prostitutes' fault they ended up how they did. She saw them sometimes, leaning out of the windows of the saloon, smoking cigarettes and drinking at all hours of the day. When they turned away from their customers, they looked exhausted and unhappy.

"So, you're not screwin' the sheriff and you weren't robbin' him. So what were you doing there?"

"I was looking for the sheriff, same as you," Penelope said sweetly, the wheels in her head turning. Her identity might be a bargaining chip, and she didn't want to give it up too quickly.

"And you didn't find him?"

"Wouldn't be here if I did, would I?"

Mell let out a little *hmm*, eyeing Penelope speculatively. "You know the sheriff well?"

Penelope kept her face carefully blank. "Everyone in Fortuna knows the sheriff."

"Well, I know him too. I know he's a damned dirty liar." A storm cloud passed over Mell's face.

"Hey," Vera said, all the cockiness gone as she laid a hand on her captain's shoulder. "We're going to save Corinna. You know we will."

Corinna. Currier's little sister. The one who was supposed to hang. Penelope gulped, her thoughts flying to the documents she'd hidden in the sheriff's office. It was good she'd left the papers where she did, instead of slipping them into her pocket where Currier and her gang might find them. Something was off about Wiley's testimony in the Currier case, but a man was still dead. She needed more information before she decided what to do with the papers she'd found. And it looked like she was in the right place to find that information. Penelope sat up a little straighter, an idea brewing.

Mell shrugged Vera's comforting hand off her shoulder and turned back to Penelope, her eyes blazing. "You know why we're after your darling sheriff?"

"Sure. All of Fortuna knows," Penelope said, forcing nonchalance into her voice. "He arrested you."

"We've been arrested loads," Mell snapped. "Wiley Barnett *lied* on the stand."

Now they were getting somewhere. "You're saying you didn't rob all those people?"

Mell snorted. "Oh, we robbed them all right."

"Then I guess the sheriff was just doing his job."

"He said my baby sister killed that man, that mayor. But she didn't fire a shot in that ambush!"

"'Ambush'?" Penelope said, raising her eyebrows. "Is that what you call storming a town?"

"We were in White Hills for supplies. We *paid* for those goods, just as we've done a million times over. Your precious sheriff is the one that started that gunfight, not us."

That was news to Penelope. The papers she'd found in Wiley's office said the bandits had attacked the town. "He was protecting the territory," Penelope countered, wanting to see what Currier would say. "Everyone knows that."

"Yeah, he's a big hero, isn't he?" Mell said sharply. "Lying to a judge and sending a girl who's not yet eighteen to the gallows."

"She's not going to hang," Vera cut in stubbornly. "We're gonna get Barnett to recant."

"By kidnapping him?" Penelope asked.

"If we have to," Vera said darkly. "Corinna didn't kill that man, and none of the rest of us did, either."

Penelope narrowed her eyes. "Then how'd he end up with a bullet in him?"

"That's exactly what we'd like to ask the sheriff," Mell said.

Penelope frowned. None of it added up. *Someone* had murdered the mayor of White Hills, after all. She hadn't believed Wiley's account of what happened, but how could she believe these women? They were criminals. The throbbing bump on the back of her head attested to that.

"People get caught in the cross fire when idiots with hero complexes start a gunfight in the middle of a busy town," Mell said. "But Corinna wasn't *in* that gunfight. I hid her away the second the bullets started flying. The only reason Barnett was able to pin that shooting on her was because no one had seen her all day."

"So you don't know for sure she didn't do it."

"Of course I do," Mell said fiercely. "She told me so." Her brown eyes blazed and her small stature seemed to melt away—she looked larger than life and more than capable of causing damage.

Penelope shrank back. "Look, I'm not accusing your sister of anything," she said quickly, holding up her hands.

Mell narrowed her eyes consideringly. "I never did get your name, sweetheart."

Penelope considered lying. She had no idea how Currier would react if she knew she had Wiley's fiancée in her grasp. But Currier didn't seem to know that the sheriff even had a fiancée. "Penelope."

"Penelope. Okay. And who is Penelope? You some farmer's wife?"

"She said her father would pay for her release," Vera said helpfully.

"Father? Not husband?" Mell asked sharply.

Penelope felt her cheeks flush at the interest in the bandit's eyes. "I'm not married."

Vera's smirk turned mean. "Bit old to be unmarried," she said with a snort, sticking out a booted toe to poke at the hem of Penelope's skirts. "No man'll have you?"

"I could say the same to you," Penelope said angrily, drawing back.

"Oh, I've had *plenty* of men," Vera laughed.

"We *know*, Vera." Mell rolled her eyes. "So. Unmarried . . . somehow," Mell said with raised eyebrows, the last word coming out under her breath. Her gaze dragged over Penelope. "At what? Thirty?"

Penelope gasped, scandalized. "I am twenty-six." Generally, she thought she looked pretty good for her age. For years, she'd been telling herself she could pass for younger.

"Hey, no offense meant," Mell said, holding up her hands. "So. Penelope. Twenty-six. Unmarried. Father who might pay your ransom." Mell ticked the points off on her fingers. "You got anything else to tell us that might make you useful?"

Penelope hesitated. On the one hand, her head ached fiercely, and she knew she was in more danger than she had ever encountered in her boring little life before. On the other hand, this was an opportunity to get the answers that Wiley wouldn't, or couldn't, give her. She knew what a good woman would do, but she also knew what the heroes in all her novels would do. They would find out the truth. "No," she said. "But if you write to my father, he *will* pay for my release." That would give her until the morning. Surely she could survive on the ship that long?

"I don't want money," Mell said dismissively. "I want information."

"Should we dump her back in town?" Vera asked, sneering down at Penelope.

Mell shook her head. "Nah. I think we'll hold on to her a little longer. Just to see."

See what? Penelope wanted to know, but Currier wasn't being any more forthcoming.

"All right, get up," Mell said impatiently.

Penelope balked. "What for?" Images of torture swam vividly through her mind.

The bandit rolled her eyes. "You wanna sit on the floor in the storeroom? Be my guest."

"You're . . . letting me out?"

"We're on a flying ship, darlin'. I don't know where you think you're gonna run off to in the sky." Mell snorted. "So either you stretch your legs and get something to eat, or you stay in here all night. No skin off my nose either way."

"I'll come with you," Penelope said quickly, scrambling to her feet. It would certainly make hunting for information easier if she wasn't locked in a storage cupboard. At this rate, she'd probably have the thing solved by morning.

"How's the head?" Mell asked as Penelope stepped out into the narrow hall. "Ruth packs quite a wallop."

Her tone sounded almost concerned, which couldn't be right. Bandits didn't worry about the well-being of their hostages.

"It hurts," Penelope said shortly. She wasn't going to let Currier intimidate her.

Mell gave a considering hum. "We don't got much by way of medical on board, but Elsie does all right by us when we need mendin' after a fight. She can have a look at it."

"Oh. All right," Penelope said slowly.

Now that they were side by side she could see that she had a few inches on Currier's small frame. It wasn't the build of a terrifying outlaw.

The hall they stood in was narrow, but it had electric lights set into the wall to brighten up the space.

"Come on," Mell said, nodding down the length of the corridor. "Mess is this way. You must be hungry."

Penelope thought about it for a minute and found that she was. She didn't know how long she'd been out in the storage room, but she had certainly missed dinner.

She followed Currier down the passage, with Vera at her rear, stepping close behind her to remind Penelope that she was trapped. Currier, on the other hand, barely spared Penelope a glance to make sure she was following.

The sound of voices drifted through the ship, growing louder until Currier paused before a swinging door. "Here we go," she said. "The heart of the *Star*."

She pushed the doors open. The wide space had several tables and a window into what looked like a galley kitchen. Hanging chandeliers with electric lights threw sunny beams onto the walls, casting a warm glow over the scene. It was fancier than Penelope had expected.

In fact, so far nothing about the *Persephone Star* and its crew was what she had been expecting. The dazzling lights made Penelope's head spin; she felt like she'd stepped into another world, especially when she noticed the round portholes running down one side of the room, revealing nothing but the night sky and the light of the moon, the ground nowhere in sight.

VI.

Three women looked up in surprise as Mell strode through the door, Penelope at her heels.

The largest of the three flushed a deep crimson at the sight of Penelope and dropped her eyes. She had hair the color of straw tied back at the nape of her neck, and she was built like a cattle driver.

"Crew." Mell's voice carried through the room, command in that syllable. The women straightened under her gaze. "Meet our guest. Penelope."

Penelope panicked and gave a small wave. To her kidnappers.

"This is Elsie Curtis." Mell gestured at a woman wearing britches and a blousy shirt, the type the handsome traveling men wore.

"June Nichols." This woman was older than the rest and wore a respectable dress, cut high around her neck, made of simple fabric.

"And you've already met Ruth Wallace. She's the one who clocked you." Mell gestured at the giant of a woman, who appeared more and more embarrassed by the second.

"Sorry," she grunted. "I ain't known it was you, or I weren't a' done it."

Penelope clamped down on the urge to tell her it was all right; it most certainly was not, not from the way her head was still aching. But something about the big woman's childish contrition inspired sympathy.

"Now, Penelope says she's got nothing to do with anything and we should let her go home. Of course, I don't believe her, so she's going to be staying with us for a while."

"Oh, is *that* the reason," Vera muttered from somewhere behind Penelope. Penelope frowned, wondering what she meant by that.

"We've lost the element of surprise with Barnett already," Mell continued. Ruth's blush intensified. "So we may as well see if we can turn her to good account."

Penelope shot Mell a look of outrage, but the woman was turned away. What did that mean, *good account*? What would they do with her?

"Do try not to knock her unconscious again, though," Mell said with a grin. "She's crabby when she comes to."

Penelope muttered uncharitably under her breath and refused to give Mell the satisfaction of seeing her upset.

"You all right, sweetheart?" the one called Elsie asked, her accent thick as molasses. "I know Ruth can pack a mean punch."

Penelope recoiled as the woman stepped toward her, but Mell grabbed her arm and tugged her forward.

"Elsie's the doctor. Let her look at your head."

"I ain't a real doctor," Elsie said apologetically. "Seeing as I'm a woman and all. But my momma was a nurse in the war. I watched her real good."

It wasn't the most reassuring of speeches, but Elsie had wide, concerned blue eyes and so Penelope let herself be led to a nearby table. She sank down onto the rough wooden bench and tipped her head forward when Elsie told her to. The fingers that probed the bump on her head were cool and gentle.

"Skin didn't break," Elsie said. "You watch that swelling, and if it gets any worse, you come right to me, you hear? But otherwise, I think you'll be right as rain in a few days."

"Thank you, ma'am," Penelope mumbled, drawing a screech of laughter out of Mell.

"'Ma'am'! Did you hear that? Our little librarian here is a real polite one! Elsie's only twenty, though, so you'd be better off calling her 'miss' or 'doc,' like we do."

Penelope's head shot up. "How'd you know I was the librarian?" Maybe Currier had been playing dumb, and knew all about Penelope. Her eyes narrowed.

But Mell seemed as surprised as Penelope felt. "You are? For real?" She let out a guffaw that ricocheted off the walls around them. Her face opened up with the laughter, and she suddenly appeared years younger, like she was just a young woman, after all. A pretty one.

"What?" Penelope demanded. She hardly saw the humor in her profession.

"You just—" Mell snorted. "You look like one, is all."

There was absolutely nothing wrong with looking like a librarian, but somehow Penelope knew she should be insulted. She glanced down at her tidy clothes, long skirts, and neat waistcoat in bewilderment.

"Can enough people in that town even read?"

Penelope bristled but had to admit, "It's not quite a full library. I keep it in the post office, but I'm building the collection!"

The rest of the women were laughing, but Mell's face had gone sharp and considering. "You run the post office?"

Penelope clamped her teeth shut so fast the *clink* was audible. But at Mell's hard look, she muttered, "I do."

Mell was at her side in an instant. Penelope shrank back. Mell was a killer, and her posture, alert and aggressive, brought that point home. Penelope suddenly felt in over her head, and one of her few bargaining chips had slipped out of her grasp because she didn't think before she spoke. None of her heroes would have been so foolish.

"Why didn't you say so?" Mell asked, her voice dripping with false honey.

Penelope raised her chin. "What's it to you?"

"A postmaster can be a real useful thing," Mell said thoughtfully, leaning in even closer. Behind Mell's sharp eyes, Penelope could practically see the wheels turning, far too fast for Penelope's liking.

"I just give people messages."

"You don't just give the messages, darling. You read them."

Penelope thought guiltily of the messages hidden in the sheriff's office—it was certainly information Currier would want. But she wasn't going to give secrets to a criminal that easily. "What do you want to know?"

"You ever see any telegrams about me?"

"Sure," Penelope said. Mell perked up, but she continued, as blandly as she could, "We get them by the bucketful these days."

"Not those," Mell snapped. "I mean about before."

"Before when?" Penelope gave Currier her sweetest, dumbest look.

"When the ambush happened. When my sister was arrested. The trial. Anything."

"I wasn't postmistress then. I came to Fortuna less than a year ago."

Mell's shoulders sagged. "Oh. So you don't know anything about my sister?"

Penelope had heard people call Corinna Currier unnatural, a wench, a whore, and a devil. She certainly wasn't going to repeat any of that in this company.

"They're gonna kill her, you know? She's got an execution date set for two weeks from now. They're gonna string her up. My sweet baby sister." Mell's voice had gone quiet. "She didn't have nobody else to look out for her 'cept for me, but she weren't cut out for the criminal life. That's why I got her out of the line of fire when Barnett ambushed us. I promised I'd always protect her. Now she's going to hang." Mell sounded heartbroken. Nothing like the hardened criminal everyone made her out to be.

"She's not going to hang. The lawyer will see to that," June said, bundling Mell into the crook of her motherly arm. "He's appealing, and they'll have to let her go. We know the truth and so does God."

Penelope's eyebrows rose, and Ruth leaned in conspiratorially. "June's daddy were a preacher. Don't pay her any mind if prayin' ain't your thing."

"I go to church every Sunday."

"Course you do." Vera snorted. "Captain, you want me to feed her or not?"

Mell looked up, her eyes gleaming wet in the light. "Yes. Get her dinner. Give her a place to bunk."

"Fine. Let me see what's left in the mess." Vera stalked over to the tiny galley kitchen, her boots clomping with indignation the whole way.

Penelope's gaze followed the former prostitute as she rattled around in the kitchen, wondering how she'd learned to cook. It wasn't a skill Penelope normally associated with those in a brothel. But then again, she didn't know how a middle-aged preacher's daughter ended up with a bunch of criminals, or how sweet Elsie with her gentle hands had been suckered in by Mell Currier, either.

They were all a mystery—especially Currier, smaller and softer than Penelope could have ever imagined.

Everyone dispersed after that, Mell striding off, wiping fiercely at the tears in her eyes, June ushering Elsie away to set up a bed for Penelope, and Ruth grabbing the whiskey bottle that had been abandoned on the table and slinking away with all the subtley of a mastiff.

Penelope was left alone with only the sound of Vera cooking for company.

When it became clear that no one was going to hang around and keep an eye on her, she leapt up from her seat. She wasn't foolish enough to try anything, not with Vera still half-visible in the kitchen, but she couldn't stop herself from pressing up against the small porthole, craning her neck to try to see the ground below them. They were over desert. It stretched wide and flat and dry around them, its magnitude making it hard to judge how high in the sky they really were.

She'd heard that airships docked against skyscrapers back in New York, buildings that rose a hundred and fifty feet into the sky. It was hard to picture, but it got slightly easier as Penelope peered out the window at the world below.

"Here."

Penelope jumped. Vera stood behind her, one hand on her shapely hip and a plate in the other.

"Don't go wanderin' around," she said gruffly. "You might break something." She set the plate on the table with more care than Penelope had expected and then turned on her heel and headed back into the kitchen.

Penelope looked down at the offering with surprise. Potatoes dripping in butter, fried chicken, and a pile of fresh beans so green they made Penelope's mouth water. She hadn't realized how hungry she was until that moment.

She took a tentative bite, and then a bigger one, and then she was scarfing the food down, manners be damned.

She didn't have to worry about being ladylike in a place like this, anyway. Her gaze stole to the bare expanse of Vera's legs, visible through the doorway of the kitchen, shuffling around as she washed the dishes and hummed an upbeat tune.

June returned to the mess as Penelope was scraping her plate clean.

"She's a good cook, isn't she?" June said with a kindly smile.

"That was some of the best fried chicken I've ever eaten," Penelope admitted. June's grin turned proud.

"You wouldn't have known it when she joined up. She didn't seem to eat anything but scraps washed down with moonshine. But she wanted to learn a skill." June shot a fond look over at the kitchen, where Vera was still busy. "Wanted to be useful for something other than her body, for a change."

The older woman seemed in the mood to talk, and so Penelope hastily swallowed down the food in her mouth and took the opportunity to ask some questions.

"How did she—" Penelope began awkwardly.

"Stray from the Lord?"

"No." Penelope had a pretty good idea how that had happened. "Join up."

"Oh. We were in Bronco, Texas, for a . . . job. It was early evening, the time when men go drinking with their friends and get some bad ideas about the girls available to them in saloons." June turned sad eyes toward the kitchen. "Some townswoman got tired of waiting for her man to come home in the evening and took matters into her own hands. We saw the blaze from where we were docked, just outside of town."

Penelope gasped. "She set the saloon on fire?"

"Yup. Place went up like a powder keg, what with all the alcohol inside. Mell jumped right up and pulled her gun like she was gonna shoot the fire down." June shook her head with a sad little laugh. "When we realized what had happened, Mell got us into town. There wasn't much we could do when we got there, though."

The idea of Mell Currier running toward trouble wasn't surprising, but the idea of her racing to help strangers certainly was. "She wanted to help?" she asked skeptically.

"Course." June nodded sagely. "We could see it was the saloon. Mell knew there'd be girls inside, and no one was gonna worry about getting them out, except maybe the man who held their contracts. Vera was outside when we got there. She was—" June shook her head again, words catching in her throat. "She was on fire, and weren't nobody doing anything to help her. She was screaming."

Penelope clapped a hand over her mouth, her eyes darting toward the kitchen. "What happened?" she squeaked.

"Well, Mell dumped a barrel of water right out of the sky, put her out instantly. Then she went racing down there, screaming at everyone who was there for not doing anything to help. Some men, who were a bit worse for the fire themselves, said some unkind things to her in the heat of the moment about the worth of a prostitute. One of them was more upset because his horse got caught by the blaze."

Penelope felt sick.

"Mell brought Vera on board then, because she could tell no one was gonna get her to a doctor, not when there were *respectable citizens* with burns." The vitriol was clear even in June's gentle voice. "She stayed after that. Said we couldn't get rid of her even if we wanted to—which we never have."

"Is she—" Penelope started, stealing another glance toward the kitchen. "Did she fully recover?"

"She's got scars from the fire. Pretty much the only places that don't got them are the places she insists on flaunting about. Said she was right glad her breasts were spared, the foolish thing." June laughed.

Penelope tried to picture it, what might be under the corset and skirt—they had seemed to show so much just a few hours before, but now it seemed like they hid far more.

"So Mell saved her," she said.

"Well, Mell saved all of us," June replied, as if it was a given.

"And now she's trying to save Corinna?" Penelope hazarded.

The corners of June's mouth tugged down. "Corinna will be fine," she said. It sounded more like she was trying to convince herself than she was Penelope. "Our lawyer will see to that."

"But Mell said . . . in two weeks?"

June shook her head emphatically. "No. It won't happen. Corinna has had an execution date set since the moment that fool of a judge convicted her. And I've fought, and I've fought, and I've gotten it pushed back. We have the best lawyer that Mell's money can buy. He'll get it pushed back again."

Penelope knew she shouldn't, but she couldn't help pressing. Just to know a bit more. "Mell didn't seem to think so."

"Mell doesn't trust in lawyers. When the girls were arrested . . ." June trailed off, her mouth twisting at the memory. "They were all locked up, and Corinna was . . . sentenced. I was on my own to deal with it. So I found the best lawyer I could persuade to work for us. What could Mell do from behind bars? And they would have hung Corinna that week if I didn't do something. But he's a man and Mell doesn't trust any man. So now that she's a free woman, she wants to solve things the only way she knows how."

"With a showdown?" Penelope whispered.

"She thinks she can clear Corinna's name before the lawyer does, by confronting your sheriff."

"And what do you think?" Penelope asked quietly, her mind fixed on the peaceful streets of Fortuna. The last thing she wanted in the world was to see them run with blood. The idea of Cathryn Houser or Elizabeth Mycock ducking for cover, of Tobias Combes having to defend himself, of Sarah, of her *father* caught in the cross fire. She couldn't bear to think of it.

June stood before Penelope could press her further. "Come on, now, let's get you to bed. I imagine it's been a bit more dramatic a day than you're used to."

Penelope followed June, her mind still caught on the image of blood running through the streets of Fortuna. Whatever else she accomplished on this ship, she had to stop that vision from coming true. Somehow.

June led her to a bunk room, the beds stacked two by two. "You'll be sharing with Elsie and Byrdie and me," she explained, shooing Penelope inside.

"Byrdie?"

"Oh, she's the one who keeps us in the air. You'll meet her eventually."

Penelope crawled into bed, her thoughts a jumble, wondering what other secrets the *Persephone Star* might hold.

VII.

The whirring sound of a medical saw woke Penelope. She bolted upright, her heart pounding, thoughts of torture and injury flooding her brain. All she felt, though, was a dull ache in the back of her head. She gazed blearily around the cabin. The faint light of morning poured past a colored shawl tacked over the nearest porthole, tinting the whole room with a rosy warmth. In the bed across from her lay June, the edges of a respectable nightgown peeking out over the blanket drawn up to her shoulders. Her salt-and-pepper hair was tucked under a sleeping bonnet, trimmed with neat lace. Above her, Penelope could just make out Elsie's face over the edge of the top bunk, her blonde hair spread over the pillow, her cheeks rosy like a child's.

Neither of them seemed at all disturbed by the grating noise that ripped through the cabin.

Penelope's brow furrowed. The sound seemed to be coming from above her, and now that she listened more closely, she could tell it wasn't the whirring of a crank bone saw at all. It was more like a pig that was dying.

Cautiously, she stuck her head out of the bunk and peered upward.

Ruth Wallace let out another snore, her mouth hanging open, her cheeks ruddy. The force of the snore seemed to shake her whole body, but she slumbered peacefully on.

Penelope stared for a few seconds, having trouble comprehending that a human being could make such a sound—let alone a *woman*.

The rest of the women must have gotten used to the sound over time, but there was no way Penelope could return to sleep with that racket buzzing in her ear. Besides . . . Penelope's eyes widened. With everyone else asleep, she was completely unguarded. This was her opportunity to have a look around the ship unsupervised. With one more cautious glance back at her bunkmates, Penelope crept quietly out of the cabin.

The hall was deserted. Penelope didn't quite know what she was looking for. A room labeled *Why Wiley Barnett is out to get us*? She shook her head with a snort and tiptoed down the corridor. She needed answers. Otherwise Wiley's anger was going to get the better of him, and another shoot-out would happen.

A second closed door suggested a cabin like the one she had spent the night in; she passed it by, wondering if the indomitable Mell Currier lay behind it. Did the woman even sleep? It seemed impossible somehow.

The next door was the washroom that she'd been hurried through the night before. Beyond that was the mess.

Penelope peeked through the swinging doors, but no one was inside. She rushed across the room and out the other side in a matter of second, uncomfortable in the wide-open space. She knew the back portion of the boat was storage, because it was where they'd stored her. She wondered what else they kept back there.

Penelope peered into the small cubbyholes that lined the prow of the boat, the rooms growing smaller as the floor sloped up under them.

She swung open a door and froze at the gleaming, glimmering interior. Weapons were stockpiled from the floor to the ceiling, every size and shape of gun and sword and bayonet Penelope could imagine. She gulped, staring at the gleaming metal, death promised by every shining surface. She slammed the door shut, leaning back against it with a shuddery breath.

The reports of the *Star* building an armory had obviously not been false. A fight was coming, and now Penelope knew it would be sometime in the next two weeks. Before Corinna Currier lost her life on the gallows.

She closed her eyes, struggling to get her breathing under control, reminding herself that this was no surprise. She knew the crew was dangerous. She knew she was in danger while she was on board. This reminder just made it all the more imperative that she find out *something* to keep the fight from coming to Fortuna. If the characters in her novels could do it, then so could she.

She turned back toward the main living quarters of the boat, forcing herself to walk sedately, as if she hadn't seen anything.

"Whatcha doin'?"

Penelope screamed.

A head poked through the ceiling, grinning at her.

Or, well, it wasn't really the ceiling, once she looked closer. Just before the mess doors was a staircase—really more of a ladder—that led up into a trapdoor.

A young woman's head hung down out of the door, watching Penelope with a grin.

"Hope I didn't startle you." She giggled.

"Oh, really?" Penelope snapped, still breathless.

The woman laughed again. Her head pulled back and disappeared, to be replaced by a pair of boots, legs, and then a torso, sliding through the trapdoor to perch on the top of the stairs. Her mischievous face peeked back into view.

"You must be our hostage," the woman said.

Penelope thought back to June's explanation of the bunking situation the night before. "You must be . . . Byrdie?"

The woman looked pleased. "Ah, heard about me, have you?" She slid down another two steps and held out a hand. "Pleasure to meet you."

Penelope shook it, marveling at the absurdity of the situation. "Penelope."

"So I heard. Everyone's talking about you, as well."

"I thought you were going to be sleeping in my cabin."

Byrdie grinned. "I was. I just don't spend all morning lazing about like the rest of you."

Penelope started. "What time is it?"

"Half past five."

"And that's lazy?" Penelope normally slept until at least eight; no one wanted her at the post office until nine.

"Sure is," Byrdie confirmed. "Ruth takes my bunk after last watch. I imagine she's what woke you?"

"I take it you've heard her sleep?" Penelope said dryly.

"Enough to wake the dead," Byrdie agreed. "Don't know how June and Elsie sleep through it. You comin' up?"

Surprised, Penelope peered up at the trapdoor. "Where's 'up'?"

"The deck, of course!" Byrdie said enthusiastically, reaching above her head to push the trapdoor wide. "Best part of the ship. Can't stay down in the brig the whole time you're here!"

She gestured eagerly, and Penelope found herself hitching up her skirts and mounting the precarious steps, as if Byrdie's enthusiasm were catching.

The woman had hair cut short, dark freckles scattered across her face, and a smile that said she'd gotten away with everything in her school days. It was a combination that was hard to say no to.

When her head cleared the floor of the deck, Penelope let out an involuntary gasp. Byrdie tipped a happy wink back at her.

"She's a beauty, isn't she?"

Penelope scrambled up onto the deck, nodding. In front of her, in the prow of the ship, was a window that rose floor to ceiling, curving around to cover more than a dozen feet of the sides of the ship as well. The lead paneled squares were cut large and the frets were small, so it felt like there was almost nothing between her and the sky.

And what a sky it was.

The sunrise hadn't quite burned away in the light of the day; the clouds around them tinted candy pink. The desert sand was lit up with an orange glow, and seemed to stretch on endlessly below them.

Penelope stepped closer, breathless.

Even back in Boston and New York she'd never been above the fourth story in a building.

Now she was unimaginably high, seeing a view meant only for the birds. It was stunning.

"Not bad, eh?" Byrdie asked at her elbow.

Penelope turned, shaking her head. "I can't believe it."

"That's what I thought when I first got up here too." Byrdie gazed out the window, her expression just as awed as Penelope felt, even though she must have seen the same sight a thousand times before.

"June said you fly the ship?"

"Sure do," Byrdie said proudly. "Used to drive delivery trucks for my father back in Brooklyn, but I wasn't sure I'd be good at this when I first tried it. Mell says I'm a natural, though. Come and see."

She led Penelope a little ways back from the window, where a large bronze ship's wheel stood. Byrdie ran a reverential hand over one of its spokes.

"On a boat—a water boat—this'd move the rudder," she explained with a smile. "But for us, it shifts the sails. Lets us steer. If we need more oomph, we've got mechanical power." She tapped a large lever next to the wheel. "Gives us a boost if the wind's not in our favor. "These"—she tapped some more toggles—"control the air in the balloon. That's how we go up and down."

"Sounds a bit more complicated than a delivery truck."

Byrdie tipped her head back with a laugh. "I guess it is. But I always liked going fast and far, even back then."

"Why'd you leave Brooklyn?"

"Nothin' to keep me there," Byrdie said.

"Not your family?" Penelope pressed. "You look so young."

"I'm nineteen," Byrdie said indignantly. Then she shrugged, her eyes on the sky. "My dad died."

"Oh. I'm sorry."

"I'd've kept driving that delivery truck forever if they let me." Her eyes went misty as she gazed ahead, into the expanse of brightening blue.

"What stopped you?"

For all she'd just met the young woman, Penelope could picture it: a young Byrdie careening down a back alley, laughing her head off as stray cats leapt out of her way and old women hollered at her to show some decorum, steam trailing in her wake.

Byrdie shot her a glance. "My dad tried to leave the business to me. But I'm a girl, so I couldn't have it. They sold it at auction. I stood at the back and watched it happen. Nothin' I could do."

"But that's stealing!"

"Oh, I got the profits. Women can inherit money, but not a business holding. Not if they don't have a husband. And I wasn't about to get married just for that truck, no matter how much I loved it."

Penelope was willing to bet that the business meant a lot more to Byrdie than just a truck, but she kept her mouth shut.

"I took a job as a driver on cross-country steam coaches and left Brooklyn," Byrdie said with a twist of her lips. "It was an okay job. I got to see a lot of the country, and that was pretty great."

"But?" Penelope asked.

"How do you know there's a 'but' coming?" Byrdie asked, the grin returning to her face.

"Well, you're here, aren't you?"

"That I am." She shrugged again, more lightheartedly. "Not much to tell. It was a fine job, but not the greatest. Some people didn't take too kindly to a girl behind the wheel, especially a teenager. Said they'd hire a different coach. Lost a decent amount of good fares that way. Made my bosses antsy."

"That's not fair."

"Nope," Byrdie agreed good-naturedly. She toggled levers and turned the wheel as she spoke, hands fluid. "But I ran into Mell on one of my runs—she was holding up the coach—"

"What?" Penelope gasped.

Byrdie laughed. "Ah, it wasn't a big deal. I had a wealthy businessman in the back, owned a line of brothels and shady liquor halls from Kentucky to Colorado. Mell had been tracking him for weeks. She robbed him blind, ran off with the contracts to a dozen girls he was plannin' on moving out to the territories, and offered me a job all in the same breath. I left that fool sitting in the coach on a dusty road in Mississippi and never looked back."

Penelope remembered what June had told her about Vera. "She got some kind of a crusade against prostitution?"

"She don't like hearing about women being taken advantage of." Byrdie said. "Lot of those girls were fifteen, sixteen years old. Mell doesn't take kindly to that kind of thing."

Penelope didn't either, but she only read about heroic rescues in novels. She'd never dare carry one out herself.

"Mell gave me all the money she took off the man," Byrdie continued happily. "Called it my first month's wages—a hell of a good month it was too."

"Why would she do that?" Penelope had always heard that Mirage Currier was gold hungry, pure and simple.

"Said I should save it in case I wanted to buy my dad's business back one day," Byrdie said, ducking her head shyly over the wheel.

"Oh. That's . . ." Penelope didn't know what to say.

"Mell's just like that," Byrdie said cheerfully.

"Mell's just like what?" a voice rang out over the deck. Penelope whirled around while Byrdie laughed. Mell stood by the trapdoor to the brig, her hands planted firmly on her hips.

The morning light shone brightly on the captain, and Penelope was struck by how, well, *striking* she was. Mell wasn't beautiful, in the typical sense, and she wasn't handsome like a man, but there was something about her. Maybe it was the confidence with which she entered every room. It was enough to leave Penelope momentarily stunned. She looked away, knowing her cheeks were pink.

"A slave driver and a tyrant," Byrdie said, tipping a wink at Penelope.

Penelope floundered, unsure how she was supposed to respond.

"And don't you forget it."

"Aye, aye, Captain."

Mell swaggered forward, regarding Penelope with a cocked eyebrow. "So, little librarian, what brings you on deck?"

"Found her wandering around downstairs," Byrdie answered for her. Penelope winced, but Byrdie continued on blithely, "Ruth's snoring drove her out of bed."

Mell let out a sigh. "Vera sleeps in a cupboard because of it."

An incredulous laugh bubbled up out of Penelope's throat, unbidden, but Byrdie shook her head. "She's not kidding. There's a bed in the bunk room for her, but Vera wouldn't take it. Said nothing in the cathouse could have prepared her for the indecency of that sound."

Penelope's face went hot. It was the kind of frank talk a woman of her standing should never hear, but darn if it wasn't a little bit funny too.

"So, what do you think of the old girl?" Mell asked. Her voice was even, but something in her eyes told Penelope she cared more than she let on.

Twenty-four hours earlier, Penelope would have been terrified of the idea of a conversation with Mirage Currier, but in the moment she only felt nervous—not that Mell was going to hurt her, but that she would think Penelope was just another small-town woman with small-town ideas. A nobody, worth nothing. So she was honest. "It's a beautiful ship. Really. I can't get over it."

"*She*," Mell tutted. "All boats are girls, but the *Persephone Star*'s a fine *woman*. Stands up for herself and doesn't let anyone push her around."

"She's Mell's pride and joy. Although, she would have fallen out of the sky by now if it wasn't for me," Byrdie said.

Penelope expected the captain to lash out at the insult, but instead Mell rolled her eyes. "Talk, talk, talk," she muttered, knocking her shoulder into Byrdie's as she came to stand next to her.

Byrdie ducked her head to stage whisper to Penelope. "Only had the old girl a year when I joined up. She had big plans to become the lady Jesse James, but she could barely steer the *Star*."

"Lies and slander," Mell said, but her tone wasn't angry. "We're meant to be inspiring *fear* in the heart of the hostage, Byrdie."

"You said I was a guest," Penelope reminded her, surprised at her own gumption.

"Either way," Mell grumbled. "We're outlaws."

"Course we are, Mell," Byrdie said soothingly. "I'm sure Miss Penelope's properly afraid."

If it was hard to reconcile the woman in front of her with the hero at the heart of June's and Byrdie's tales, it was even harder to reconcile her with the reputation of Mirage Currier, terror of the West.

"Terrified," she assured them.

Mell shot her a cocky grin. "Well, as long as you don't forget that."

But the fear was already slipping away with every smile or wink Mell tossed her way.

"Come on, librarian," Mell said. "Since you're up already, you can earn your keep." She grabbed something from the corner and thrust it into Penelope's hands.

"What's this?"

"Toolbox."

Penelope frowned down at the box in her hands. "I hope you're not expecting me to fix anything. I can't even hang pictures on the wall."

"There isn't much décor in here, don't worry," Mell said, reaching above her to lever open another trapdoor.

Penelope gaped as the ceiling above them lowered, revealing the underside of the giant balloon that kept them in the air. A gust of wind rattled past, clanking the chains that connected the ship to its mooring.

"I hope you're not afraid of heights." Mell smirked as a rope ladder unrolled into her hands.

"What if I am?"

"Then things are about to get pretty frightening." Mell laughed and climbed up *out of the ship.*

"We're a hundred feet in the air!" Penelope yelled after her.

"You better follow on," Byrdie said. "She's going to need that toolbox."

Penelope squinted through the hole in the ceiling as Mell opened another trapdoor, one that led into the balloon itself.

Penelope gasped. "Isn't that going to let the air out?"

Byrdie barked a laugh. "Don't worry—Mell knows how to keep this bird in the sky. Up you go."

Left with no choice, Penelope got a better grip on the handle of the toolbox and placed a foot on the ladder. It swayed ominously, and she closed her eyes, sending out a prayer for deliverance, before starting to climb.

The distance between the ship and the balloon wasn't great, but it felt like an eternity before Mell reached down to tug the toolbox out of Penelope's shaking fingers. With both hands free, she levered herself up into the balloon.

It was dark inside and Penelope blinked, trying to force her eyes to adjust.

"One second!" Mell called from somewhere nearby.

Lights flickered on and Penelope let out an involuntary gasp. Above their heads hung a crowd of balloons, each bigger than a coach.

"Are those what are holding us up?" Some of the balloons seemed suspiciously slack, and Penelope gulped.

"Yep." Mell grinned. "We'd be in real trouble without these babies."

"Don't even say it," Penelope pleaded, all too aware of how high in the air they were.

"Sorry." Mell looked unrepentant. "Byrdie's been having trouble stabilizing us. She reckons there's a problem with one of the balloons."

Terror swooped through Penelope's stomach.

"So, I'm just going to have a nose round and patch up whatever I can."

"And what do you need me for?"

"To hand me my tools."

"Surely one of the crew could have done that?"

Mell shrugged. "I thought you might want to see this. It's probably not a chance you're ever going to get again."

Penelope glanced around herself; Currier probably had a point.

It was a miracle of science and engineering; she knew that from everything she'd read about dirigibles. She peered closer, with more curiosity this time. The space loomed large around them, the length of the ship, and higher than a two-story building. Cladding ran along the inside of the space like the bones of a skeleton. It made Penelope remember standing in the natural history museum in New York as a child, staring up at the massive bones of a whale suspended eerily in the air above her.

Penelope looked down at the space below them, visible through the open trapdoor, a dizzying drop between them and the comforting, solid form of the *Star*. "You must really not think I'm a threat, huh?" she asked, not sure whether to be relieved or offended.

Mell squinted at her. "What do you mean?"

"Well, we're all alone and precariously high. One push, and I've rid the world of Mirage Currier once and for all."

"I can think of better things to do now that we're alone," Mell said, half under her breath. "But I don't think you want to hurt me any more than I want to hurt you."

Penelope ignored the puzzling first comment, which made her stomach flutter curiously. "Oh yeah? How do you figure?"

"I reckon we're not as different as you'd like to think," Mell said. She barreled on before Penelope could object. "Right now, for instance, we're both stuck. You want to go home and I want to save my sister. I don't think you'd push me, because I'm your best chance out of here."

"And what would stop you from pushing me?" Penelope challenged, shocking herself.

"Well, first of all, you're too pretty to die. And I'm hoping that you'll be able to help me with my problem. I just don't know how yet."

"I'm too . . . what?" Penelope spluttered.

Instead of answering, Mell set down the toolbox and began deftly scaling the wall. Small metal protrusions let her climb, moving easily like a child scrambling up a tree in summer.

"Too pretty?" Penelope whispered skeptically. She raised a hand, patting at her hair, which she was sure was little better than a rat's nest after a night on the ship. Was Mell making fun of her? She must be, but the comment still sent a little frisson of pleasure through her. She wasn't used to being complimented by anyone except the drunks that leered at her from the porch of the saloon.

When Mell was halfway up the wall, she reached out and began to examine the balloons.

"Yup!" she called down. "We got a leak!"

Penelope forgot all about Mell's comments as her heart thudded. "Is that dangerous?"

"Everything is dangerous sometimes, darling," Mell called back. "You just gotta try to get to things before they get to that point."

"And have you?" Penelope prompted anxiously.

"Yeah, yeah. We're gonna be fine. I need you to get into the toolbox and pull out a patch kit."

Penelope squatted down to rifle through the box. She found a small pouch labeled correctly and pulled it out triumphantly.

"Now just bring that up here," Mell said. A hand stuck out from behind the balloons, waving invitingly.

"What?" Penelope stared up at the looming wall. "No. I can't."

"Why not?"

"Because I'll fall and die."

"Ah, an optimist." Mell laughed. "You won't die. I did it just fine."

"You know what you're doing."

"I'll remember you said that," Mell said.

"I can't climb in a skirt," Penelope argued.

"Next time, think about wearing trousers. Now come on."

Penelope grumbled, approaching the wall. She'd told herself last night that she could be brave, but even in the confines of that tiny storage room, faced with known killers, she hadn't imagined *this*. She looked up—and up and up, to where Mell perched. Dying in an accidental fall after being captured by bandits seemed particularly perverse. Maybe Mell had planned it that way all along; maybe she killed her victims by enticing them into lunatic behavior.

Penelope set one hand on a metal loop. "I can't."

"Come on, little librarian. Haven't you ever read those novels of yours and wondered what you'd do in the same situation? Would you be brave enough to fight the bad guy, to reveal the secret, to stand up to a villain?"

"The heroes of my novels are all men," Penelope whined. But she put a foot up on a hold nevertheless.

Mell let out a *tsk* above her.

"That's because the writers are all men, and they lack imagination. Don't let them tell you what you can and cannot do. They write nice little ladies who stay at home and make soup just to convince us that it's all we can do in life."

"Soup?" Penelope said incredulously, but she began to scale the wall. One hand over the other.

"Sure. Or a roast. I don't know, Vera does the cooking. But if your novels tell you that only men can do heroic things, then you're reading the wrong kind of books."

"Says the woman who decided to be a villain, not a hero."

"Only according to the men who make the laws."

Penelope frowned. The law was the law, wasn't it? But June and Byrdie had both insisted that Mell was a hero. Was she really only a bandit in the eyes of men like Wiley?

Wiley might have been the sheriff, but he didn't exactly represent law and order. Certainly not when he looked the other way for one of his friends, or deputized a bunch of disorderly drunks.

"There we go."

Penelope was shocked to see she had come level with Mell already. "That wasn't so hard!"

"See?" Mell said. "I expect you could do a lot if you put your mind to it."

Penelope flushed and ducked her head, fumbling for the bag of supplies. "Here." She thrust it out across the space to where Mell perched among the air bags, secure on the rigging that held them in place.

"Aren't you coming over here?"

"Are you crazy? No, what am I saying? Of course you are. You're *Mirage Currier*." Penelope shook her head. "It's too far."

"I'm just plain Mell. And you said it was too high, too. And yet here you are."

"You got me this far. Can't you just be satisfied with that?"

Mell chuckled. "If I was ever satisfied, I wouldn't own this here boat."

Penelope clung tight to the handholds as Mell fiddled with the patching tools. "How *did* you get this ship? You can't be much older than me."

Mell let out an indignant noise. "Hey! I'll have you know I'm *much* younger than you."

Penelope turned slightly, frowning skeptically.

"I'm twenty-four."

"Oh, my mistake. You're practically a child," Penelope teased.

"I knew you'd see it my way. What with all the wisdom of age..."

Penelope flushed red. "You . . .!" Mell's smirk cut her short. "You take that back!"

"Make me," Mell trilled, swinging farther into the mass of air bags.

"I see what you're doing," Penelope warned, but still, she considered the distance between them. It wasn't as far as she'd first thought. Maybe four or five feet to the rigging. Her arms stretched that far, with a bit of a reach. "Maybe I will."

Mell peeked her head back around one of the balloons, her eyes twinkling. "Maybe you should."

Penelope took a deep breath. She could do it. Mell had done it, and she was a woman, just like Penelope. There was no reason she wouldn't make it to the balloons just as easily.

"Okay," she said resolutely. "Here goes nothing."

She squeezed her eyes shut and swung out, one hand and one foot safely on the handhold, the others flailing wildly into the empty space beside her. The reality of how empty and how deep that space was hit Penelope like a punch to the gut, and she let out a desperate noise.

"You've got it." Mell's voice was steady and sure.

The thick texture of the rope brushed her fingers, and Penelope grabbed hold. With one more deep breath she pulled, tugging her weight over, away from the safety of the iron under her fingers, the solidity of the wall of the balloon, and into the ether.

She cracked an eye open.

Mell's smiling face was much closer than before. Penelope could see a dimple that threatened to peek into view in Mell's left cheek. "You did it."

Penelope glanced down. She hung in the rigging, higher up than she wanted to think about, but the large ponderous presence of the balloons somehow made her feel safe. "I did." A smile split her face, so wide it burned.

"That's the spirit." Mell held out the pouch Penelope had carried up. "Now hold this."

"Oh, I see how it is," Penelope spluttered. "Menial labor, that's all you want me for."

Mell shot her a sidelong look. "Well, it's one use for you, that's for sure."

The comment brought color to Penelope's face. She fumbled with the bag, holding it open so Mell could reach inside. Mell found what she wanted and swung back to the leaky balloon. Penelope watched her work, her hands quick and methodical. It wasn't that different from stitching a shirt or a quilt, yet one was deemed "woman's work" while the other was "mechanical," so surely only a man could do it. But Mell was woman enough, with her petite frame and curves that her tight trousers did nothing to hide. Her mouth, pursed in concentrated, was as plump and pink and kissable as any girl's, Penelope thought, her eyes sweeping over Mell while the captain was distracted.

"Hand me the doohickey."

Penelope started, feeling caught out. "Oh yes, the *doohickey*. Of course. From the Latin for 'I don't know what you're talking about.'"

Mell leaned around the balloon she was repairing to sneer. "The tool thing."

"Are you sure you're qualified to be doing this? Byrdie probably knows the actual name for these things."

"Oh, sure," Mell drawled, turning back to her work. "You like Byrdie better than me. Is it the freckles?"

"The what?" Penelope snorted.

"Oh, don't pretend you don't know. She's adorable. When we rob banks the tellers practically chuck her under the chin."

"Well, that must be useful."

The mention of crime didn't send the expected frisson of terror through Penelope. She thought about what Byrdie had told her. "You give a lot of that money away?"

Mell swung back around to arch an eyebrow at her. "Why? You need a loan?"

"No! I just. Byrdie said..."

"Oh. *Byrdie* again." Mell shook her head. She reached out an insistent hand, and Penelope pressed the pliers into her palm. "We do give some away," Mell admitted quietly.

"Why? I mean, you must want the money, or you wouldn't take it."

"Do you know how those banks work?"

Heat burned at Penelope's cheeks. She knew the inner-workings of a bank better than almost anyone. She'd been dandled at the knee and at the account books, raised on how to best make a profit.

"I have some idea," she said.

"Men run them, asking you to hand your hard-earned money over to them, to do God knows what with. They buy and sell with *your* dollars. And then when you need a bit back, when the crops have failed or your husband died, or your kid got sick and the medicine has to be shipped from goddamned Philadelphia, those same bank men don't want to know you. Sure, they've been using your money for years, but you need a hand? Sorry, this isn't a charity." Mell pursed her lips. "It's not right. Widows lose their homes, children don't have enough to eat, and the bank man goes home with his pockets bulging."

Penelope had seen Ashes foreclose on houses, had seen her father give a loan when he didn't think it would pay off, and then sell off the property a year later to the highest bidder. He wasn't trying to hurt anyone, but people did get hurt.

Mell stitched the patch on with quick, capable hands, in and out and in again. Each puncture of the needle sent a jolt through Penelope, still half-worried the whole ship would go crashing down to earth. But it seemed Mell knew what she was doing.

"So, who do you give the money to?"

"Those widows. The children. The women who gave their inheritance over to a deadbeat husband who risked it all on a bad gamble." Mell stuck the needle in her mouth, deftly tying off the thread. "It's not so bad these days, but I heard stories 'bout the Rush. While I was young still, it was all anyone talked about out here. Who made it big, but more often than not, who lost everything." She handed the needle back to Penelope. "Men came out here, speculating on what they didn't got, but more often than not they dragged people with them. Families got wrecked by gold lust. I still see it—not only in the mining camps, but everywhere. Everyone out here is trying to make money quick, and no one's succeeding but the bank robbers."

"No one but you, you mean."

"Yeah, I do. I take the money from people who don't earn it, and I try to make sure those kids eat right for a while. Or I help women buy coach passage back to their families in the east. The Wild West isn't for everyone, little librarian."

Penelope knew that better than anyone. "Don't call me that," she said morosely.

"Why not?"

She sighed. "It's not a real library."

Mell peered at her. "What do you mean? It's got books, don't it?"

Penelope bit her lip. "No one wants to borrow them."

"Why not? Ain't that the point of a library?"

"Everyone thinks it's silly, having a lending library in a cowpoke town. Some of the townsfolk can't even read, and the ones that can don't read much more than the newspaper."

Mell gestured with the pliers. "That just means they really need a library," she said sensibly. "Maybe you could do readings, or something. Get them interested in a book, and then tell them they can take it home with them."

"That's . . ." Penelope faltered. "That's not a terrible idea."

"Or, you know, the magazines print books in them. I mean, chapters of books. I hear people wait around at the newsagents, dying to get their hands on the next installment. Maybe you could do that?"

Penelope knew about serialized books. Dock workers flooding the streets to hear the new work of Mr. Dickens back in the '40s and '50s. But she was surprised someone like Currier paid attention to those kinds of things.

Fortuna didn't have a newspaper—they made do with news from other towns, primarily White Hills, which was large enough to have a press. But she wondered if she could distribute a chapter of a book for free from the post office, and hope people got interested.

"People laugh at me when I try to make the library work," she said with a sigh.

"What people?"

"My fi—father."

"That's terrible," Mell said decidedly. "If he cares about you, he should support what you do."

"He used to. When I was little. He used to tell me that I could do anything I put my mind to."

"But not anymore?"

"Now he tells me I shouldn't do anything a lady wouldn't."

Outrage blossomed on Mell's face. It was cute, almost. "That's such bullshit."

"Ah, ah. That would be one of the things a lady doesn't do," Penelope said with a weak chuckle.

"Bull*shit*," Mell repeated with relish. "And what about the things a *father* shouldn't do, huh?"

"Does your family support you?" Penelope asked bluntly.

"My family's Corinna," Mell said, dropping her eyes back to her work. "We always support each other."

Penelope bit her lip, flooded with guilt. She didn't have anyone but her father, and even though they'd grown distant from each other, she would always help him if he were in trouble. And she could help Corinna. She wouldn't even have to give the evidence to Mell. If she told Mell about the papers, maybe Mell would be able to save Corinna. Would it be so wrong to tell her where to look in the sheriff's station?

The second the thought crossed her mind, Penelope blanched. Would it be so bad to send her into Fortuna, armed with the suspicion that its sheriff had played dirty? To send a *killer* where her father was? Where innocent people were? No, she could never do that.

So she tried to steer the conversation away from Corinna and her own guilt. "How did you end up out here?" How did someone so young and so seemingly normal end up as Mirage Currier?

"My mother was one of those widows. Not the ones taken advantage of by the bank, exactly." Mell tucked her chin over one of the ropes, as comfortable as if they were on land. "We came out west, like so many other families. Gold was all anyone talked about back then—I'm sure you remember."

Penelope nodded.

"We were all going to become rich. Never mind the heat, and the distance, and the disease, and the natives..."

"So you're not—" Penelope stopped, embarrassed.

"Part Hopi?" Mell smiled. "No, not by blood. They're good people, though. They've been more hard done by than anyone else out here, and that's saying something. All the natives. It makes me sick to think what we've done, for land or for gold. For God and country." She shook her head.

"I think the rumors started because I went to them once after I got shot." She tapped her thigh with a hearty *thwack*. "We'd been trading for a long time, building up relations. And no doctor in the territory was going to treat me. The Hopi took me in. They're incredible people."

Mell's face was entirely earnest, and Penelope realized she had never given the tribes much thought. More guilt bubbled inside her.

"They don't deserve any of what's happened to them. But no one does."

Mirroring Mell's posture, Penelope sank onto a rope, draping her arms over the next rung. It was almost comfortable, swinging there above the world. "But what about your family?"

"Hmm? Oh. My father died, and my mother tried her best, but she died too. And then it was just me, Corinna, and June."

"Wait, June? As in—"

"She was our—I don't even know the word. She was our everything. Not a governess, not a servant—not by a mile. She took care of the whole family, and she looked after me and Corinna. She was always with us."

"So that explains it," Penelope said under her breath.

Mell's laughter echoed through the chamber. "What? A good Christian woman among a bunch of outlaws?"

"Well . . ."

"She's a good woman, but don't let her fool you. She wants to look out for me and Corinna. But she believes in what we do as much as the rest of us."

"And that's . . . crime?" Penelope hazarded.

"In one sense of the word. But June doesn't see it that way." Mell said speculatively. "It's illegal, but June answers to a higher power."

"And the Bible is all right with what you do?"

"Yes and no, I suppose." Mell laughed. "I wasn't much for my Sunday school, although June filled in some of the gaps. But the Bible says the rich men aren't getting into heaven. Like a camel through a needle's eye, I think it says. So I figure I'm doing them a favor."

A laugh burst forth from Penelope's throat. "That's one way to look at it. What does June say?"

"She sees what the Bible don't. She sees suffering, and I guess most of all, she sees Corinna and me."

Grief flashed over Mell's face, intense and visceral, and it hit Penelope like a punch to the gut. "What was it like?" she blurted.

Mell seemed surprised. "What?"

"The ambush. I'm not fishing for salacious details or anything," Penelope said quickly, thinking of Wiley's accusations.

"'Salacious details,'" Mell repeated, bemused. "You're funny, little librarian."

"I just can't imagine what it would be like . . . to be involved in something like that."

"It was scary," Mell admitted. "We didn't expect it. I mean, of course we didn't. Or it wouldn't be an ambush." She met Penelope's eyes. "I'm good with a gun. I'm not going to pretend I'm not to protect your delicate sensibilities."

Penelope bristled. "My sensibilities aren't that delicate."

Mell's lips twisted. "Good to know."

Penelope was tiring of blushing around the young captain, but that didn't stop the heat in her cheeks.

Mell continued. "I have shot men, but only when they were doing something so monstrous that I had to. I shot a man once who was beating his child to the point of death. I feel no remorse. But I try not to use my gun. We were in White Hills for supplies and nothing more. We go into Copper Creek every week, and we're on our guard, but we don't expect to meet no trouble."

"But you got trouble in White Hills."

"We were just unloading the coach." Mell paused, closing her eyes. She gave a quick shake of the head and continued. "We had goods to sell as well as buy. We were getting everything out, peaceful like, when a bullet dug deep in the door of the coach."

A shiver ran through Penelope. She could imagine it, the whizzing sound through the air, the shock of the puncturing wood, the splinters flying as the bullet burrowed in.

"I threw Corinna behind me. I always keep her—" Mell stopped, swallowing "—kept her on the ship when we was going anywhere dangerous. But she wanted to do some shopping and it wasn't supposed to be risky. Not just going in for supplies."

"Then what happened?"

"There were bullets raining down. More than a few men stationed around White Hills' Main Street. You could tell they planned it." Mell frowned, looking impossibly young. "We had weapons, of course. June wasn't with us, thank God. So we mobilized quickly. I kept Corinna with me. Ruth covered us with the Winchester, and I tried to get Corinna somewhere safe." She gave another shake of the head. "I was only thinking about bullets, not about nooses."

The urge to comfort her was so strong, Penelope actually reached out, her fingers hovering awkwardly between them. Luckily, Mell's eyes were closed, lost in the memory of that day. Penelope snatched her hand back.

Mell opened her eyes, pain clear in their dark depths. "I found an alley. It had some crates in it, stuff to hide behind. I pushed Corinna down and went to guard the entrance. It was a tiny thing, that alley. I knew I could hold off anyone from the main street.

"Corinna was crying. I could hear her behind me. She was trying to be quiet, but it was the same sound I'd grown up with. A kind of gulping, hiccupy noise. She was worried about us, not about herself. I wasn't going to leave her, not for anything, but then I heard Vera."

Moisture shone in Mell's eyes. "Vera's been through . . . some things. I couldn't leave her any more than I could leave Corinna. So I ran out into the street." She closed her eyes, dropping her chin. "I left my sister."

Penelope's heart clenched at the anguish in her voice. "To go to another one. It was the right thing to do."

"You think so?"

"June told me about Vera. I think you did what you had to do."

"I ran out into the street. Vera had been grazed. She was bleeding but not bad. But once I was in it, there was no getting back to Corinna. I was hunkered behind the general store porch. Men was firing out of windows, from left and right and above. I couldn't even keep track of my crew. I just stuck it out, shooting back when a shot came toward me and hoping we all got out of it alive."

She sighed. "We did, but in handcuffs."

"All of you?"

"All of us who was there. June and Byrdie were in the sky, like always. But Elsie, Ruth, Vera, Corinna, and I were dragged in. I can't tell you how relieved I was. Vera was swearin' up a storm, calling those men every name in the book, and Ruth was red with fightin', but Corinna was there, and fine. Not a scratch on her."

The relief was still there in Mell's voice, and Penelope ached for her, knowing what was going to come.

"We got hauled up before the judge, and I told him that we weren't trying to cause no harm, but he pulled up a list of offenses a mile long, from way outside of the territory."

"All true?"

"Sure. But they never have the whole story."

Somehow, Penelope believed it.

"So there I am, arguing and arguing, and on the second day this *deputy* shows up, a man I ain't never laid eyes on before, to tell the judge he seen Corinna shoot the mayor. I didn't even know the mayor was dead."

"Was that all the evidence they had?"

"Your sheriff said he saw it too. Said she took aim, deliberate like, and killed him while he ran to cover. I don't even know why he was on the street in the midst of all that. I wouldn't wish it on anyone."

"So, just Sheriff Wiley and Deputy Greenman saw it?" Penelope said, her mind racing. The papers she found made it clear that Lewis hadn't been in White Hills on the day of the shoot-out, so he couldn't have seen Corinna shoot the mayor.

She remembered the telegram from Wiley, asking Lewis to back him up. So the real question was: why would Wiley need Lewis to lie about what he saw?

"That's what I said. They're lying, but everyone believed them and not us. And now, in two weeks they're going to . . . she'll be . . ." Mell pressed her lips together hard, shaking her head against the tears that sprang into her eyes.

Guilt ate at Penelope. She should say something. She should tell Mell about the papers. She didn't know what had happened in that street, but there were only so many reasons Wiley would need Lewis to back up a bogus story for him, and none of them were good. And she couldn't get the image of Corinna's young, scared face printed on the front page of the newspaper out of her head.

"I—" she began, but then closed her mouth sharply. What would Mell do if she told her? What if she took all those gleaming weapons in her arsenal and went after Wiley? Straight into Fortuna?

Suddenly a wavering smile broke over Mell's face. She bumped her shoulder against Penelope's. "Thank you."

Penelope gave a guilty start. "For what?"

"For listening, I guess."

"I doubt you've got a lack of people to listen to you."

"Yeah, but none of them are upstanding citizens like you, little librarian."

Penelope didn't feel upstanding in that moment. She felt like she was helping to hang Corinna Currier. But she had to protect her town.

"Come on," Mell said, interrupting her thoughts. "Let's get you back on solid decking."

"Nothing solid about a ship dangling in midair," Penelope countered, watching the way Mell effortlessly swung herself off the rope and over to the handholds on the side of the balloon. The easy grace of it was admirable, even as the distance below them made Penelope's belly swoop.

"Ah, don't take that tone with me. You ain't a landlubber. Not anymore."

"No?" Penelope shifted on the rope she sat on, turning herself toward where Mell stretched out a helpful hand. "One night on board is all it takes?"

"More than most men out there have done, anyway."

"I doubt men are ever allowed on the *Star*."

"Not as free men, anyway."

"But I'm not a freewoman," Penelope reminded her.

A frown flitted across Mell's face. "About that."

Penelope couldn't stand to hear Currier express sympathy or sorrow, so she did the only thing she could think of. She swung her body forward on the ropes she still clung to, desperately reaching out for the metal rungs on the wall.

Mell laughed delightedly as Penelope clapped a hand down upon cold metal. "Yes! Now jump!"

Penelope let go, swinging wildly in the air for a moment before she found purchase on the rungs, her feet scrabbling desperately at the metal. When the air stopped rushing in her ears, she realized she never could have fallen; Mell had grabbed her tight, wrapped around her back and bracketing her to the wall.

"Thanks," she said shakily.

Mell's arm tightened around her waist for a brief second. "I wouldn't let you fall, little librarian." Her voice was low and warm in Penelope's ear.

Penelope gasped as the gust of hot breath on her sensitive skin sent an involuntary shiver down her spine. She froze, unsure what to do or say.

In a split second, Mell released her and scrambled down the ladder. "Come on! It's easy from here."

"I'll show you easy," Penelope muttered, but she followed Mell, her hands and feet sure.

IX.

Penelope's mind was reeling. The story Mell told had been contradicted by Wiley, by the lawmen in White Hills, and by the judge that sentenced Corinna. Mell was nothing but a criminal, who openly admitted that she thought she was above the law. Yet, what reason did she have to lie to Penelope? There was nothing to be gained from convincing one lone woman—who seemed to have no connection to Wiley or Corinna's case—that her sister was innocent. There was absolutely no reason to waste time and energy on a nobody like Penelope.

Unless Mell's story wasn't part of some larger nefarious plan, but was just the simple, honest truth. But if that was the case, it implicated Wiley and Lewis—and maybe every lawman in White Hills—in knowingly sending an innocent girl to the gallows. Despite her dislike of the man—and Penelope was starting to realize that she really did dislike everything about her fiancé—Penelope didn't want to believe Wiley capable of such a thing. And it was near impossible to imagine Lewis Greenman as part of some well-planned conspiracy. And why would they do it? Sure, Wiley despised the whole lot of the gang, but Corinna seemed to be the last one he'd go after. Mell said she stayed on the ship during every crime, meaning she wasn't just innocent of the murder, but also of every other charge lobbed at the crew of the *Star*. Why target her?

Nothing made sense. June, Byrdie, and most surprisingly, Mirage Currier herself, were all *kind*. Even Vera, Penelope suspected, had been kind in her own way, through the food she cooked for Penelope. Criminals were not supposed to be *nice*. Murderers shouldn't be *caring*.

"Why are you being so nice to me?" Penelope blurted, after they were back on solid decking.

Mell looked over at her, surprised. "What do you mean?"

"I'm a hostage. You kidnapped me."

"Unintentionally," Mell reminded her.

"Still. I'm pretty sure you're supposed to be keeping me under lock and key, feeding me scraps of dry bread and dirty water."

Mell barked out a startled laugh. "I was going to see if I could rustle up some breakfast for us, but if you'd prefer dry bread and bilge water..."

"You know that's not what I mean," Penelope huffed.

"Well, why wouldn't we be nice to you?" Mell countered. "You've never done anything bad to us."

The words soured in Penelope's gut. Every second she kept her mouth shut about what she knew, she *was* hurting Mell. She knew she had to do something to fix this.

"Now come on. Seeing as you don't want dry bread, why don't I fry us up some breakfast?"

She led Penelope through the doors of the mess and gave her a gentle push toward a table.

"I thought Vera did all the cooking," Penelope said.

"You implying I can't fry bacon?" Mell said, narrowing her eyes in mock outrage.

"I don't know. Can you?"

"You better believe it," Mell said, pointing a spatula at her, face serious. "Prepare to have your mind blown."

It would be hard for a simple breakfast to be more surprising than Mell herself. At every turn the captain defied Penelope's expectations. She had expected to suffer on board the *Star*, to put her life in danger in order to discover the truth about that day in White Hills. Instead, she was actually enjoying herself. Enjoying the company of Mell Currier.

While the captain clattered about in the small kitchen, Penelope propped an elbow on the table and gazed around, trying to memorize the details of the ship. Not in the hopes of learning the *Star*'s secrets, or so she could report back to the proper authorities, but because she wanted to sear the details into her memory—the sunlight trickling through the portholes, the gentle swaying of the ship, the soft sound of Mell humming in the kitchen—so she could look back on it in the years to come. Nothing that happened next was going to be simple, but for this one second, Penelope could feel the simple pleasure of flying through the open skies.

"Madam."

A plate dropped in front of Penelope, startling her out of her reverie. It had rashers of bacon and fried eggs—nothing fancy, but it still looked good.

"Thank you."

Mell grinned at her, the warm morning light catching her face and making it glow. Penelope met her twinkling eyes and felt something hot curl in her belly. She opened her mouth—to say what she didn't know—when they were interrupted by the door clattering open. Ruth strode into the room, her big work boots clunking loudly over the floors.

"Morning, Captain! Morning, prisoner," she said cheerfully, levering herself onto the bench beside Mell. "Is there breakfast?"

"If you want to make it yourself." Mell cupped an arm protectively around her own plate.

"Aw, Captain, you know I'm no good in the kitchen." Ruth pouted. "My momma was always lashing me for burning everything."

Mell's face clouded and she quickly handed a piece of bacon to the other woman. "I'll get Vera up and in the kitchen."

Ruth grinned, munching happily, as Mell strode out of the room. Penelope instinctively turned after her, and then chided herself.

"Are you going to stay, then?" Ruth asked, watching Penelope.

"Stay?"

"With the *Star*."

"Here?" Penelope's eyes widened. The idea had never occurred to her. "No! Why would I do that? I'm a hostage."

"I guess," Ruth said with a shrug. "But most women we take on board end up staying."

"I'm not like . . . other women. I don't need saving."

"I didn't need savin' when I joined up," Ruth said placidly.

Penelope eyed the other woman; she could see why Mell would want her on the crew. Unlike Byrdie or Elsie or Mell herself, Ruth was no petite girl. She had been more than capable of knocking Penelope over the head and carrying her back to the *Star* like a sack of potatoes.

But despite being big as a bear and strong as an ox, Ruth didn't seem particularly villainous. She didn't seem greedy—except for Mell's bacon, which she was steadily picking off Mell's plate—or violent, or wicked, or any of the other traits Penelope expected in an outlaw. She mostly just seemed nice and a bit slow.

Penelope leaned across the table, lowering her voice slightly even though they were the only ones in the room. "You don't exactly seem like the criminal type."

Ruth hesitated, apparently unsure how to take that. "I can be a good criminal," she finally hazarded.

"But do you want to be?"

Penelope believed Mell when she said they gave the money they stole to people who needed it, but they still did steal. Ruth was probably a wanted woman across the West. She could understand how Mell, with all her indignation at the injustices of the world, convinced herself it was worth it, but Ruth seemed different.

"We help people," Ruth said, and she sounded a lot surer about that. She started in on Mell's eggs. The captain wasn't going to have a breakfast left by the time she got back.

"Did Mell help you?" she asked gently.

Ruth nodded. "I didn't want to be stuck on a farm all my life," she said, with a vehemence that surprised Penelope. "There weren't no man that was gonna marry me, not with me lookin' the way I do. My momma always said if I had half a brain a man might make a good farmer's wife outta me, but that I was too stupid to keep house, and too ugly to warm someone's bed."

"Your *mother* said that to you?" Penelope said, aghast. She didn't remember much about her own mother, except for a sweet, gentle voice and soothing words murmured in the dark. Mothers were supposed to take care of their daughters, that much she knew.

"And my poppa. My brothers." Ruth shrugged. "My brothers went off and got married and I stayed on the farm, plantin' and tendin'. Herdin' up the cattle. Choppin' wood, mendin' fences. It seemed like it would go on forever, and I'd never see anything except my parents' farm. Then Mell showed up."

"She offered you a chance to see the world?"

"I don't know about the *world*," Ruth said practically. "But I seen a lot more than I would have in Elk City, Kansas."

There was a clattering in the corridor, and Mell swept back into the mess hall. Ruth glanced down at the empty plate in front of her and the tips of her ears turned red. "I, uh . . ." she spluttered.

"Save it, Wallace. Vera will make me something else."

Ruth glanced down at the plate again and then looked up hopefully. "Will she make me something too?"

"One breakfast not enough?"

"It was barely one breakfast," Ruth protested. "There weren't even potatoes!"

Mell barked out a laugh. "Fair enough. O'Brien! Ruth wants potatoes."

"Is that an Irish joke?" Vera demanded as she swanned into the mess with Elsie and June at her heels. She had on a dress today, a high neck but a skirt even shorter than the one she'd worn the day before. Her boots ran up to her knees, and Penelope wondered what the skin looked like underneath that tough leather.

With the five women in the mess, the room suddenly felt alive. They filled up the space with their chatter and laughter, more raucous than any quilting circle or church social Penelope had ever attended.

Vera ranted about the state Mell had left her kitchen in, and Ruth called out hopeful suggestions for what they should have for breakfast. Elsie teased Mell for being unable to control her crew, and Mell responded by throwing napkins at her, making her giggle and duck beneath the table.

In their midst, June just sighed, raising her eyebrows at Penelope in sympathy.

They didn't exactly inspire terror, and Penelope felt more sure than ever that, whatever their crimes, it wouldn't be any kind of *justice* to hang them for it. Not Ruth, with her slow certainty in Mell's mission, or June, gazing around the room with maternal fondness, or Vera, sniping at most of them but feeding them with all the care in the world. Not Byrdie, up on deck with her eyes and her mind in the clouds. Corinna couldn't be so much different from these women that she deserved what was coming to her, even if she *had* pulled the trigger. What had Mell said? That there was what was right, and there was the law—and those weren't always the same thing.

Penelope couldn't go on pretending she didn't know anything. She had to say *something*. But what?

"Should Ruth and I still do the supply run?" Elsie asked in the midst of the chaos. "Now that we've got . . . an unexpected guest on board?"

Mell frowned thoughtfully, then glanced over at Penelope. "Do you reckon anyone's looking for you yet?"

"They will have been searching since last night," Penelope admitted.

"Of course they would," June said, reaching out to pat her hand. "Most of us, we don't have family to speak of. Not outside this ship." Something passed through her eyes, sad and dark. "We tend to forget about them."

"It's just my father, but I'm sure he's terrified about what happened to me. They've probably worked out who took me."

Mell frowned at Ruth. "It was supposed to be a stealth mission."

"Nobody saw me, I told you! I came right back, even when I realized I got a woman instead of a man."

"They'll have put it together anyway," Penelope pointed out. "You're the only thing anyone talks about in Fortuna these days."

"Really?" Mell looked pleased.

"Does that mean someone'll be coming for you?" June asked.

Penelope thought about it. Her father would have sent a messenger into town to see if she got held up, or decided to have the evening meal with a friend. When word came back that no one had seen her that evening, he would get worried. He'd come into town himself, check the post office. Find Wiley.

Then there would be a search party. Criminals haunted the roads in and out of town, but Wiley's first thought would be Mell.

"Probably," she said reluctantly.

Mell frowned again. "Who do you got that's brave enough to track you *here*?"

Penelope thought of Wiley's violent anger, and the reckless barbarity of the posse he'd assembled. No, fear wouldn't keep them away. "They'll send the sheriff," she said, voice flat.

"That's not bad, is it?" Ruth asked. "We wanted the sheriff anyway."

"We wanted him off his guard and alone," Mell huffed. "Not to have him breaking down our door with a posse at his back."

An idea was starting to form in Penelope's mind. She knew she needed to tell Mell about the papers. It wasn't a secret she was willing to keep. But she also wasn't willing to send Mell into Fortuna. Once Mell and Wiley met, bad things were sure to happen, and Penelope *wouldn't* put her townspeople in harm's way. But what if she brought Fortuna to Mell? Or, at least, the part of Fortuna that mattered? What if instead of telling Mell about the papers, she told her about Lewis? *Someone* would be coming for Penelope; she was sure of that. But did it have to be Wiley?

"I know you wanted Sheriff Barnett," she said quickly, before she could talk herself out of the idea. Mell glanced up, confused. "To interrogate. But I know the sheriff—everyone in Fortuna does. He'd never tell you anything."

Mell's expression turned fierce. "I'd make him."

"I'm telling you, he wouldn't talk. Pride matters to him more than anything."

"So what? Am I just supposed to give up and let my sister die?"

June reached out and put a comforting hand on Mell's arm.

"No. You should talk to Deputy Greenman."

Now Mell seemed lost. "What?"

"You said he's the one who testified against Corinna."

"Him and the sheriff, that's right," Mell said slowly.

"So he must know as much as the sheriff does," Penelope said, her thoughts on those telegrams. "But you won't find two men on God's green earth more different than the sheriff and his deputy. Lewis Greenman doesn't have a spine to speak of. You ask him a difficult question or two, and I'm sure he'd tell you everything you needed to know."

The whole gang looked gobsmacked, except for Ruth, who was only had eyes for her eggs.

"Are you . . . helping us plot against your lawmen?" Mell asked.

"You sound pretty sure she didn't do it," Penelope said firmly. "If that's true, then getting her out is the right thing to do."

"What's right don't keep people from hanging," Mell said bitterly.

"Deputy Greenman is a good enough man. I think he'll help you."

Lewis wasn't any good at lying; Penelope had seen that firsthand. She was sure the meek deputy would crack under the pressure of interrogation and tell Mell everything. And then everything would be out in the open. If there had been wrongdoing, if something had been wrong about Lewis's testimony, they would find out directly from the source.

"Even if we kidnap him?"

Penelope's eyes widened. "I didn't say that! No, I want you to trade me for him."

"What?"

"You said I might be of some use," Penelope said with a little shrug. "And someone is going to come for me, one way or another. So write to Sheriff Barnett and tell him you'll let me go, but only if they send Deputy Greenman to fetch me—alone."

"Why would you help us?" It was Elsie, surprisingly, who asked the question, her wide blue eyes narrowing suspiciously.

"You said it yourself," Penelope said, addressing Mell. "I'm an upstanding citizen." She turned her gaze to the rest of the gang. "I don't want to see an innocent girl hang."

Elsie pursed her lips thoughtfully. "That's mighty good of you."

Penelope didn't feel very good, but she hoped that she was starting to do the right thing.

"Are you *sure* you don't want to stay on?" Ruth asked. "You're better'n me at this stuff."

Mell laughed. "Has Ruth here been making you offers?"

"I only said that most people stay," Ruth objected.

"Yeah, but the librarian ain't most people. She's not suited to this kind of life."

The words were said kindly, and Penelope knew they were true, but they still stung. She had kind of been hoping that Mell would repeat Ruth's invitation.

"So what do you think?" she asked, reminding herself that she was there to do what was right, not join a criminal gang.

"You think the sheriff will do as we ask?"

"Hopefully he'll think this is you being cowardly—too afraid to face him."

Mell frowned fiercely, but Penelope knew she would have to admit the wisdom of it. If Wiley didn't feel challenged, he wouldn't feel the need to charge in, guns blazing.

"Well," Mell said after a moment. "I suppose it's worth a try. And I would like to ask that yellow-backed little deputy some questions. All right." She smacked her hands down on the table enthusiastically. "Elsie, you'll go to town as planned, but make a detour at the post office."

"Penelope should go with her," June put in.

"What?"

"Unless he's an even bigger fool than I think, the sheriff will be sure to question the postmaster after he receives our telegram. If he's seen Penelope, then that's proof we've really got her. And he'll be able to tell the sheriff that she's hale and hearty."

Penelope hadn't reckoned on being *that* involved in this conspiracy against Fortuna's sheriff's office, but she had to admit that June had a point.

"June," Vera huffed. "She's a hostage! She'll run away if we let her off the ship."

"No, I won't!" Penelope said indignantly. "Why would I? I'm the one who came up with this plan!"

"Maybe you came up with the plan just to trick us into taking you back down to solid ground," Vera countered, crossing her arms defiantly.

"Penelope didn't suggest she be the one to send the message," Mell said reasonably. "That was June's idea."

Vera walked over to the captain and tugged her aside slightly. "You can't possibly trust her!" she hissed, her words all too audible in the quiet of the room. June shot Penelope a sympathetic look.

Mell glanced at Penelope, her eyes thoughtful. "You know, I think I do," she told Vera.

Vera threw her hands up in surrender. "Fine. But I hope I don't end up saying 'I told you so.'"

"It's not nice to lie, Vera," Mell said with a laugh. "You're absolutely hoping you get to say it. But I don't think you will." She turned to

Elsie. "Penelope will go with you and send the telegram herself. But take Ruth along too."

"What for?" Ruth asked.

"For Vera's peace of mind." Mell met Penelope's eyes. "Ruth'll make sure you don't try anything, won't you Ruth?"

The big woman was surprised, but then nodded solemnly. "Sure, Captain. If you say so."

The ache in Penelope's head attested to how well Ruth could keep her in line. "Fair enough," she agreed.

"But you can't send her like that," June cut in.

Penelope turned to her, surprised. "Like what?"

"Well . . ." June said, obviously searching for the right words.

"Like you got walloped over the head, stuffed in a storage cupboard, and slept in your clothes," Elsie cut in bluntly.

"Oh." Penelope glanced down at herself. Sweat stiffened the fabric of her shirt and dirt clung to the folds of her skirt. Her face heated, wondering just how terrible she looked. Mell hadn't said anything earlier—in fact, she had called Penelope pretty. Now Penelope wondered if she had been teasing Penelope about what a state she was in, especially when Mell walked around looking like *that*, like it took no effort at all.

But Mell frowned and said, "She looks fine."

A small smile came to Penelope's lips unbidden.

"We want her to seem hale and hearty, remember," June said gently. "The telegrapher will hardly report that when she looks like we've been making her sleep in a cell somewhere."

"Okay, okay," Mell said with a laugh. "I'll get her cleaned up." She plucked a piece of bacon off the platter in the middle of the table. "Come on, little librarian. Time to play dress up."

Penelope scrambled up after her, leaving the rest of the women to their breakfast. It *would* feel good to get her dirty clothes off, though she wondered what kind of a wardrobe they had to offer her on board the *Star*.

Mell led her back to the washroom and pushed open a door that Penelope hadn't noticed the night before. Inside was a disarray of clothing; it was clearly the wardrobes of the whole crew mixed together.

"You're taller than me," Mell acknowledged ruefully, "so I don't think my gear'll fit you." She swept her eyes over Penelope. Her gaze was speculative, taking stock of Penelope's measurements, but that didn't stop Penelope from blushing, feeling the weight of Mell's eyes on her like they were hands running up and down the length of her body.

"Elsie's things might fit you, if you don't mind showing some ankle?" She turned to rummage through the wardrobe.

"Oh!" Penelope glanced down to where her long, respectable skirt nearly brushed the floor. "I—I'm not sure," she stammered. She knew some men got downright excited by the sight of a well-turned ankle peeking out from beneath the hem of a lady's skirt. Looking at the subtle curve of Mell's legs within her tall boots, the way they tapered to show off her slender ankles, Penelope could almost understand why.

"Well, just give them a try," Mell said. Penelope snapped her eyes back up to Mell's face with a guilty start.

She reached for the garment Mell held out, their fingers brushing within the folds of the fabric. A soft smile crept onto Mell's face.

Penelope's own smile dropped from her face as she shook the garment out in front of her. "These are *trousers*," she gasped, nearly dropping the offending article.

Mell arched an amused eyebrow. "So?"

"I can't wear these." Penelope pushed them back at Mell almost frantically. Mell wouldn't take them.

"Why not?"

"Because they're *trousers*."

"Yes, I'm aware."

Penelope let out a huff. "Ladies don't wear trousers."

"Are you sayin' I ain't a lady?" Mell asked with a laugh.

"You most certainly are not." Mell was a woman, all right; the lissome lines of her body in her fitted clothes, which Penelope found it hard to tear her eyes from, made that *very* clear. But she wasn't a lady.

"I'm going to take that as a compliment," Mell said.

"You can take it any way you want, as long as you also take these," Penelope said, thrusting the trousers at her.

"Oh, come on, librarian! Live a little!"

Penelope thought she was living plenty, conspiring against her fiancé with a bunch of bandits. Not that she could say that to Mell.

"I can live just fine without flaunting my legs for the whole world to see."

"What if it was just for me to see?" Mell asked, voice dropping low. She took a tentative step toward Penelope.

"What?" But the image burned into Penelope's mind. Slipping into the soft fabric as Mell watched. Rolling them up her legs like a pair of stockings and feeling Mell's eyes slowly drag up with them. Her face flamed.

"Okay, okay," Mell laughed. "Don't get your petticoats in a knot. You look like you're going to faint. Give them here."

"I— What?" Penelope said again helplessly, as Mell snatched the britches back. The image hadn't quite cleared from her mind, and heat stirred within her. She shifted uncomfortably.

"You should try them one day, though, little librarian," Mell said, turning back to the cupboard. "You've never felt so free as when you first get into britches."

Penelope thought maybe she'd had too much freedom lately, for all that she was still technically a hostage. Her mind certainly felt free to conjure up all kinds of confusing images.

"If it was a no to the britches, should I assume you also won't want any of Vera's stuff?"

"Of course not!"

"Shame," Mell said, glancing back over her shoulder. "I think you'd look mighty interesting."

Penelope planted her hands on her hips. "If you just want to laugh at me, I can find my own clothes."

"Oh trust me, I wouldn't be laughing." Mell's eyes were heavy, and the heat within Penelope flickered hotter.

"But they wouldn't suit you," Mell continued lowly, stepping away from the cupboard and toward Penelope. "You're too pretty for that gaudy stuff. You'd want something as soft and lovely as you are." She reached out, brushing a curl back from Penelope's face. The touch was as light as a feather, but Penelope felt it like a brand.

"I—" She faltered, at a loss for words. It came out as a whisper. She could see warm flecks the color of the desert in Mell's dark eyes.

Mell's thoughtful expression turned rueful. "We don't got much that's soft and lovely up here, I'm afraid." She took a step back.

"I don't need soft," Penelope blurted, hardly knowing what she was saying. "I mean. Whatever you have. I'll take whatever you have."

"Really?" Mell asked.

Penelope was fairly sure they weren't talking about clothing anymore. "Really."

Mell gave her a long, considering look. "There's a lot more to you than people might think, little librarian."

"I'm going to take that as a compliment," Penelope said, turning Mell's words back on her.

"Oh, I meant it as one. I bet your townspeople don't know the half of how interesting you are."

It was true that none of them—the ladies gossiping in the general store, the men kicking their heels up in the saloon, Wiley stalking the streets, or her father sitting contentedly in his luxurious office—none of them would be able to believe the things Penelope had been doing for the last twenty-four hours. She hardly recognized herself.

Mell turned back to the mélange of clothes, and Penelope instantly missed having the captain's eyes on her.

"I think being up here has made me more interesting," she said boldly.

Mell snuck a peek at her over her shoulder. "Nah," she said with a smile. "You were already interesting. We're just giving you the opportunity to show off how much."

The words warmed Penelope in an entirely different way than the heat that had flamed through her a minute before.

"Here," Mell said after a moment of sorting through the cupboard. Her voice had gone oddly quiet. "You may be tougher than you look, but you still deserve something pretty." She turned, holding out a soft pink dress.

It was girlish, a delicate calico with a simple white collar, meant for someone far younger than Penelope. She'd look a bit silly in it, but it was far preferable to the other garments she saw peeking out of the cupboard.

"Where did this come from?" she asked, finding it hard to picture any of the crew wearing it.

"It's Corinna's," Mell said softly.

"Oh!" Penelope gasped, pushing it back at Mell. "No, I can't take that!"

"Course you can. It'll suit you. You're tall, like she is."

"But—" It felt sacrilegious to even touch the dress, kept so carefully in the hope that Corinna would be released.

"I want you to be comfortable, little librarian," Mell said. "You'll be unhappy in everything else we got."

"I can make do," Penelope said, nearly ready to resign herself to trousers if it would flush the sadness from Mell's eyes.

"That's what I've been trying to tell you," Mell said. "You shouldn't have to 'make do.' If something doesn't suit you, you should change it."

Once again, Penelope knew they weren't talking about clothes. "I'm trying," she said, thinking about Wiley, and Lewis, and the hidden papers.

"I know you are. Your library is proof of that. Now, get dressed. I want to see how much that pretty dress suits you." She smiled at Penelope, but didn't leave the room.

"Oh— I—" Penelope faltered. They were two women, after all. Back east, Penelope had had a lady's maid, who helped her into her clothes every day. This felt different. Her hands came up to the pearly buttons on her dress. She plucked the top one open, revealing a small sliver of her pale throat.

Mell's eyes widened. "I'll just leave you to it, then," she said quickly, a faint splash of pink dashed across her cheeks. She stopped at the door, but didn't turn back. "Unless you need help?"

Would she turn back if Penelope said yes? Her hands had looked so quick and capable mending the tear on the balloon. What would they feel like on Penelope? Prying the buttons open, sliding the fabric off Penelope's shoulders, skimming down the length of her arms. Would they catch around her waist as the fabric pooled at her feet?

"I can manage," Penelope said, voice husky.

Mell nodded once, not looking back, and slipped out of the room.

Penelope looked down and immediately wished she hadn't.

"Are you sure this is safe?" she squeaked, squeezing her eyes shut tight.

"Haven't had any accidents yet!" Elsie replied cheerfully. Penelope groaned.

They were in a small steam-coach, swaying in a surprisingly brisk wind, as it was lowered tortuously to the ground. The pulleys above them moaned and creaked as the coach descended, and Penelope didn't want to think about how they were constructed, or how old they were, or the last time they had been checked for safety.

She focused on a spot in front of her, refusing to so much as glance at the window again.

The steam-coach was smaller than the one that sometimes came through Fortuna, but Penelope was still impressed. No one in Fortuna owned their own, not even her father, who looked at the ones that passed with envious eyes.

The coach hit ground with a bump, jarring out the breath Penelope had been holding.

Byrdie's assurances of safety, as she clipped the large chains to the rings mounted on the sides of the coach, hadn't done much to ease Penelope's heart out of her throat.

Ruth lumbered out of the coach to unhook the chains that dangled a hundred feet from the sky, while Elsie slipped out to plant herself up on the driver's seat.

The ride to town was short. Copper Creek was Fortuna's closest neighbor, but Penelope had only been to the town once before. The coach from Arkansas to Fortuna had stopped there, letting off the last passenger that had shared the back of the coach with the Mosers. An elderly lady, moving to be with her last remaining child. At the time Penelope had been surprised the woman had even survived the journey west; the stifling heat of Arizona had felt like it was pinning her to the leather seat. She had looked out the window at the dismal, clay-colored ground and wondered what her life was about to become. It seemed like she had traveled to the ends of the earth, following her father, following gold, with no prospects of her own to ground her.

She was no less worried rolling into Copper Creek this time.

Her exchange with Mell had left her flustered, so much so that she was having trouble concentrating on the real problems ahead of her. She kept thinking about the weight of Mell's eyes on her, the way her gaze had narrowed in on Penelope's fingers as she started slowly unbuttoning her dress.

It wasn't how women were supposed to look at other women. But then again, Penelope was pretty sure her thoughts weren't in line with how women were meant to think about other women, either.

The coach stopped outside the general store, pulling in alongside a line of horses tethered to the post. The animals started at the whirring of the engines, snorting hard, their eyes rolling to show white as they shied away from the noise. Copper Creek was too small for the horses to have adjusted to mechanical noises. Penelope started too. She needed to think about her plan, not about Mell. The real anxiety, the one she should be focusing on, was the telegram she was about to send. Would it work? Would Wiley actually listen to her for once?

Elsie hopped down from the driver's seat, cooing soothing sounds.

The commotion drew a face at the store window; the man's eyes widened and he disappeared in a flash.

The next moment, Penelope saw people creep out of the back of the store and hurry away down the street.

The coach door swung open and Elsie leaned against the frame, cocking her hip. "Ruth'll go with you to the post office," she said. Her voice was sweet, but her eyes were wary. "Mell trusts you, but . . ."

"I don't mind," Penelope assured her. "Whatever makes you feel better."

"You're a real odd hostage, you know that?" Elsie said, eyes contemplative.

"I'm trying to help."

"Yeah. That's what's odd," Elsie said, then shrugged. "I'm going to do the shopping in the meantime. If we spend too long hanging around town, the people get jumpy. Start to look kind of mob-like, if you know what I mean." Elsie turned to the larger woman, dropping a few coins into her outstretched hand. "Ruth, walk her to the office and pay the man for the telegram, all right?"

"Do I got to make sure of what she's writing?" Ruth asked with a frown, her cheeks tinting red. Penelope had seen that kind of shame scrawled across many people's faces in the post office; reading was not a much-taught skill this far west.

"No, sweetie, that's all right. You just make sure the man reads the message out at the end, okay?" Ruth relaxed as Elsie shot Penelope an apologetic look. "I just want to make sure."

Penelope expected nothing less.

Ruth clambered out of the carriage and offered Penelope a hand. The move emphasized the fact that Penelope hadn't laid eyes on a man since her capture. The crew all fulfilled the roles that she traditionally associated with men: driving coaches, doctoring, heavy lifting.

Penelope placed her hand into Ruth's large calloused one and let herself be helped to the ground.

She glanced into the window of the general store, and caught a glimpse of that day's newspaper, the same *White Hills Herald* that they read in Fortuna. She stopped, startled. *When will justice be served?* the headline demanded, over the same picture of Corinna that she had seen back in Wiley's office. Elsie followed her gaze and winced.

"Justice," she said with a scowl. "She didn't shoot anyone."

"We're going to get justice," Penelope said. "*Real* justice."

"Mell always says justice don't work for folks like us," Ruth said.

"We'll make it," Penelope said determinedly, thinking about what else Mell had said: *"If something doesn't suit you, then change it."*

"I'm glad I grabbed you by mistake," Ruth said, and then blushed. "I mean. I'm not glad I *hit* you. I just—"

"It's okay," Penelope laughed.

"You're just nice, is all."

"I think you're nice too," Penelope said.

Her words brought a childlike smile to Ruth's face.

"The oddest hostage," Elsie said with a shake of her head as she turned for the general store.

The post office was tucked at the end of the row of shops, and Penelope dutifully followed Ruth to the door. The postmaster quaked as they entered the office.

"We need to send a telegram," Ruth announced, dropping the coins on the counter.

"To whom?" the postmaster asked in a small voice.

"The sheriff's office of Fortuna," Penelope cut in, stepping up beside Ruth.

The man obediently handed over a piece of paper.

It was odd meeting him like this; Penelope felt like she should know him. They had exchanged more than enough messages over the past nine months. But they were only the conduits for the words; he didn't recognize her, and she didn't recognize him. It made no difference to him that someone else now sat at Penelope's desk in Fortuna. Henry O'Connor's boy filled in for Penelope whenever Ashes insisted she accompany him out of town. Messages that went through Jim O'Connor came out half-garbled, but Ashes still hoped the boy would take over full time when Penelope married Wiley. The fact that Jim was only fourteen, and desperate to get out of Fortuna, didn't seem to make any more difference to Ashes than the fact that Penelope had no intention of retiring.

The poor boy was probably already at his wit's end today, hauled in to cover her post and keep an eye on the news from Copper Creek; her message certainly wouldn't help.

She wrote in careful block letters:

Sheriff Wiley,

I am being held captive by the crew of the Persephone Star. *They will release me to Deputy Greenman. He must come alone. Send no one else.*

Penelope Moser

"You sure?" the man asked when he took the form back. "That's awfully long."

The formal tone cost money, but she wanted to make it clear to Wiley that she hadn't revealed their relationship to Mell. He'd be less likely to come in with his guns blazing if he didn't think this was a personal attack against him.

"We're sure," Penelope said firmly.

Ruth leaned in. "I need you to read it out, to make sure it's right."

"Okay." The postmaster's eyes widened as he repeated the message. When he had finished, he turned his frightened, searching gaze on Penelope. She could see the wheels turning in his head: What was he supposed to do with a hostage in his post office? Penelope didn't know what she'd do in his shoes, and didn't fault him for the fact that he did nothing. It was the postmaster's job to pretend that he didn't see the words on the page, after all.

"I'll get that right to Fortuna," he said, his voice shaking.

"You do that," Penelope said, tapping the counter before turning to follow Ruth back to the coach.

"Wait!" the man called out, and Penelope winced, worried he was going to attempt some heroics after all.

But all he said was, "Your post." The letters trembled as he held them out across the counter to Ruth.

Elsie was lounging next to the coach, her arms crossed carelessly, but her eyes alert. "All set, ladies?"

"Telegram sent," Ruth reported.

"Would you mind driving us back, Ruth?" Elsie asked. There was an edge to her tone.

Ruth looked a bit nonplussed, but nodded. "If you want me to, Doc." She hauled herself up onto the front of the coach.

Elsie yanked the interior door open and gestured Penelope in, her movements more urgent than her tone. "After you."

Penelope didn't hesitate to scramble inside.

Elsie locked the door behind them and gave the roof a thump. "All set, Ruthie!" she hollered.

The coach whirred to life, a puff of steam whistling out of the funnel, rushing around the windows in a hot blast.

"Everything all right?"

"Hmm?" Elsie dragged her sharp gaze away from the window. "Oh. It's nothing for you to worry about."

"But there is something?"

Elsie gave her a tight-lipped smile. "Just a man. As usual."

"What do you mean?"

"Haven't you ever had a man treat you badly because of what's between your legs?" Elsie asked bluntly.

Penelope's eyes widened. "Not—not really?" She remembered Wiley's harsh words, the way he manhandled her whenever he felt like it. But . . . he was her fiancé. That was his right.

"Well, you're luckier than most, then." Elsie shrugged. "A lot of men think every woman in the world wants their attention. You add trousers to the mix, and you end up with someone's hands on you."

Penelope looked down at the offending garment. She was surprised to find she was already getting used to the sight of them.

"Then why do you wear them?"

Elsie huffed. "Because I'm my own person. Men don't get to decide what I wear. I'm not going to pretend to be someone different just because they want me to—just to fit in."

Penelope had the sense that Elsie was talking about more than some man in the general store. "So what did you do?"

"Told him to keep his hands to himself." She smiled coldly. "Might have sprained his wrist."

Penelope's jaw dropped. "For touching you?"

Elsie leaned forward, eyes intent. "What would you do if a man touched your rear without your permission? You're a nice girl, right? You come from a nice family, you're going to have a nice husband. Girls like you don't let cattle rustlers feel what you've got under your skirts, do you?"

"Well, no. Of course not." Penelope shook her head. Men leered at her sometimes—of course they did—but everyone in Fortuna knew that she belonged to Wiley, to Ashes. They wouldn't touch another man's property.

"Not all girls are as lucky as you. They don't got a nice father to protect them. Men touch them and they think they have to let them. Men catch them alone in alleys and haul up their skirts, and they think there's nothing they can do about it."

Penelope winced. She had read about it in books. She knew it happened. Rape. It was such an ugly word. Such an ugly idea.

"Now maybe that man in the store will think twice about touching another girl just because she's small and alone."

"Did anyone help you?"

Elsie pursed her lips. "The store owner pulled a shotgun—on me. I help myself."

Penelope remembered what Ruth had said over breakfast—that the *Persephone Star* saved people.

"Is that why you joined Mell?" Penelope blurted. "To help people?"

Elsie shook her head. "I could barely help myself when Mell found me."

"What do you mean?"

The coach sped down the dusty road, the heat of the late morning pouring into the dim interior. Elsie's face was half in shadows as she spoke.

"Oh, just the usual story. I had a husband. He believed in discipline." She hunched further back into the shadows. "I was half-dead when Mell found me."

"What do you mean, a usual story?" Penelope asked, aghast.

Elsie huffed out a frustrated breath. "Men hit their wives, Penelope. More men than you probably think. No one does anything to stop them."

She sounded so jaded. "You're only twenty."

"I got married at sixteen."

Even in the small farming communities that Penelope and Ashes had passed through on their way west, most girls didn't marry until they were out of their teens. Maybe it had been young love for Elsie, a childhood sweetheart.

"How old was your husband?" Penelope ventured.

"Thirty. He was a friend of my father's. Later he told me he'd had his eye on me for years. Not that I needed telling. He was always around, watching me."

Penelope tried to picture it. A smaller, younger, more naïve Elsie, slipping behind her mother in the kitchen, or busying herself with schoolwork, while a grown man's gaze burrowed into her from across the room.

"Did you love him?"

"How could I?" Elsie laughed hollowly. She turned her face toward the window, the bright sunlight catching against her goldenrod hair. "The marriage was just a transaction between my father and my husband."

Penelope looked down at her hands. Elsie's situation sounded awfully familiar, even though Penelope was supposed to be a grown woman.

"Why do you want to know, anyway?" Elsie asked.

The contrast between the dim interior of the coach and the bright sun outside, the whirring of the engine, made Penelope feel cut off from the world, like what she said wouldn't matter, like the words would dissipate like the steam in the air around them.

"I have a fiancé," she blurted.

Elsie raised a questioning eyebrow. "Do you love him?"

"I don't . . . I don't know." She thought of Wiley's sneering face. His explosive temper. His insistent hands.

"Then why are you marrying him?"

"You know why," Penelope said. "It's . . . my father."

"It never changes, does it?" Elsie sighed. "I used to think that if I'd been older, something might have been different. But we're taught to do what we're told, to behave, to be good girls. I don't know if I could have said no to my father even if I was a decade older."

"He would have been so disappointed," Penelope said in a small voice, feeling foolish.

"Hey." Elsie sat forward urgently. "Don't marry the man if you don't love him. Please. Even if your father won't forgive you. It's not worth it."

"What happened? With your husband?"

Elsie leaned back. "He was a drunk. A mean drunk. He didn't like the way I cooked or how I made his shirts. The house was never clean enough. I never made the budget stretch the way he wanted me to. It's not an interesting story—just another woman trying to cover up the bruises when she goes into town. Your man, he doesn't?"

"He's never hit me."

"Mine didn't until after we were married."

"He wouldn't—I don't think—" Penelope cut herself off helplessly. Sometimes she was frightened of Wiley. Sometimes he was mean. Sometimes he bullied her. But she didn't think he would hit her—her situation was nothing compared to Elsie's. It was ridiculous to even bring it up.

"Even if he doesn't. Don't get stuck with someone you don't want."

"What happened to your husband?"

Elsie smiled, that same cold smile from before. "He beat me until I couldn't stand up. Until I was worried I was gonna die. He left me lying there on the floor and went to get himself another drink." Her smile widened cruelly. "He didn't even think of the shotgun propped by the door."

"You?" Penelope's eyes widened.

"I'm a wanted woman in Pennsylvania. I didn't join the *Persephone Star* to save people—I joined to kill as many bastards like my husband as possible."

Penelope hunched back into the seat. Elsie had seemed like the sweetest of the crew. A nurse, there to help people.

A foot nudged her ankle. She drew back with a sharp breath, her gaze flying up to meet Elsie's smirk.

"I'm not some kind of a mass murderer, you know. As long as you're not a man beating on his wife or kids, then you're safe from me."

"I didn't think—"

"It's all right to be scared," Elsie said, her tone gentling back into that of the sweet doctor. "Life is scary. But when I woke up in a bunk on the *Star*, my face a mess, my ribs broken, and realized that I was free—free from my husband, from my parents, and from the law in Pennsylvania—I decided to stop letting fear rule my life. You should consider it."

"I'm not afraid," Penelope insisted.

She wasn't. She felt stifled sometimes, trapped in Fortuna and trapped in her engagement, but she never felt afraid.

"Good." Elsie gave her a satisfied smile. "As long as your deputy shows up, we'll get you home in no time, and you can go back to your nice life. But think about what I said about that fiancé of yours. The rest of your life is an awfully long time to be stuck with someone you don't love."

"I'll . . . think about it."

Elsie nodded and turned her face toward the window, her eyes on the sky.

XII.

Mell was there to greet them when they got back aboard the *Star*, her anxious face peering in through the coach window.

"Everything go all right?"

Penelope scrambled from the coach, glad to be out of the stifling interior. Elsie descended more slowly behind her.

"I sent the telegram," she confirmed.

Mell closed her eyes and let out a long breath. "Good."

Penelope gave her a small smile, and her heart leapt when Mell returned it.

"This will work, right?" Mell asked, her words barely above a whisper.

"Yes," Penelope said as confidently as she could, hoping she was right.

"Oh, there's post for you, Captain," Ruth called out.

Mell looked over with a smile, but it fell as her gaze landed on the letters in Ruth's hand. Striding over, she snatched at an envelope with an official-looking wax seal, tearing it open with shaking hands. The ripped envelope fluttered to the floor.

"No. No!" The first word was a whisper, the second a scream. It tore through Penelope like the winds that raged across the desert. Mell's face had gone a deadly white.

Footsteps clattered through the ship, and June flew into the room. "What? What is it?" she asked with motherly concern.

"We lost the appeal." Mell's voice shook.

"Oh, honey." June bustled up to draw Mell into her arms. "Don't let it get you down. We'll file another one. We always do."

"No, you don't understand," Mell said, shaking her off and brandishing the letter. "We *lost*. They're going to hang her at dawn on Monday."

For a moment, June didn't seem to understand. "But." She shook her head. "No, that can't be right. It's Friday now." She looked at Mell with wide eyes. "It's *already* Friday," she said with more urgency.

Mell pulled out her pocket watch with trembling hands. "That's right. They only left us... six hours to file any new paperwork."

"But it'll take us four hours to even get to White Hills," Elsie broke in with horror.

Mell closed the watch with a *snap* that made Penelope jump. "Which leaves two hours to get a stay of execution, *without* the lawyer."

The hopelessness of the situation descended like a weight over the room. Penelope felt like she was choking on it.

"We'll—we'll figure something out," June said, but her eyes were wet with tears.

"I don't need to figure anything out," Mell said fiercely, crumpling the letter in her hand and dashing it to the floor. "I'm busting her out of there. *Tonight*."

"What?" Penelope gasped.

Mell turned to her with surprise, like she'd forgotten Penelope was in the room. She shook her head. "I'm sorry, little librarian. We'll put you down on the ground here before we go." Then she turned to her crew. "Elsie, run and tell Byrdie to turn the boat around *now*. She's to go as fast as she can without running out of fuel—we'll need to make a quick getaway on the other end."

"Got it, Captain!" Elsie said and ran from the room.

"Ruth, get Vera and head to the armory. We've been prepping for a showdown, not a jail break, so you need to take stock of what we've got and what it'll do against a thick stone wall, if it comes to that."

Ruth nodded like the orders made sense. Penelope couldn't believe what she was hearing. "What? You're just going to blast the prison wall open?"

Determination chased the tears out of Mell's eyes. "If that's the quickest way to get my sister out, then yes. *Now*, Ruth. I need to know if we're stopping for supplies on the way."

Ruth gave a clumsy salute and lumbered out of the room.

"June, you'll need to be ready to let the hatch down when we come runnin', all right?"

"Whatever you say, Mell."

Penelope couldn't believe it. Was *no one* going to stop this?

Mell glanced over at Penelope again. "Be ready to be on the ground in fifteen minutes."

"What are you going to do?" Penelope demanded.

"Get ready to kill every person who stands between me and my sister," Mell snarled, and stormed from the room.

For a moment, Penelope just stared after her in shock. Then she turned pleading eyes on June. "You're not going to let this happen, are you?"

June was weeping quietly, tears running down her wrinkled cheeks. "I don't see what else can be done. We can't let them *hang* her."

Huffing out a frustrated breath, Penelope chased after Mell. If no one else was going to stop her, she would.

"Mell, *Mell*," she called frantically. "Wait!"

Mell turned at the sound of her voice, surprised. A strange look came into her eyes; something like hope and resignation mixed together. She let Penelope catch her.

"Penelope. I wish we had longer," she said, half-frantic. "But it's not safe. You have to go."

In a swift movement, she cupped Penelope's face and dragged her lips down onto her own.

The kiss was desperate. Wet. Needy. Mell pushed against her until Penelope hit the wooden planking at her back. Mell kissed like the world was ending.

And wasn't it? Everything Penelope thought she knew, everything she was sure about, had come crashing down around her over the last few days. And so she opened her mouth and let Mell in.

The first slide of Mell's tongue was electric. Penelope shook in her grasp, panting into the kiss. She tried to kiss back, fumbling, hardly knowing what she was doing. All she knew was that the wet glide of their lips together made her feel things she hadn't thought possible.

Mell's heart thumped against her own rib cage, like it was trying to burst out of Mell's chest and burrow into Penelope. Mell bit at her open mouth, teeth catching at the plump flesh of Penelope's lip. Mell's hands ran frantically over Penelope, agile fingers catching at the dip of her waist. The touch set every nerve on fire.

Penelope didn't know how long Mell held her there, pinned, squirming against the wall. But eventually she pulled back.

"I didn't think you had it in you," she said in wonder. Her voice came out low and rough.

"I—" Penelope shook her head. She could barely say what had happened, what had come over her.

"I'm sorry it had to end this way," Mell said, and darted back in for another quick press of their lips. "But we'll be out of the territory by tomorrow night, and on the run." She shook her head ruefully. "Goodbye, Penelope." And then she turned away.

In a daze, Penelope watched her disappear round the corner. Her hand came up to her mouth, touching lips that she was sure were swollen, painted red by the force of Mell's mouth on hers. Whatever she had been expecting, that wasn't it. She shook her head, reminding herself that she had something important to say to Mell. She would worry about the kiss another time.

"No, wait!" Penelope called, pushing herself off the wall and running after Mell. The captain was in her room, pulling a chest from under the wooden bunk.

Mell looked up at the sound of her step, brow furrowed.

"I wasn't trying to say goodbye, or have a—" Her face flamed hot, and the words caught in her throat. She waved her hand, trying to indicate *everything* that had happened in the corridor.

Mell's face fell. "You weren't?"

"No! I wanted to talk some sense into you, since no one else seems willing."

"Well, then, I'm sorry," Mell said, turning back to her chest, tense. "Though you seemed to like it."

She threw open the lid, revealing a stockpile of shining weapons. Penelope's heart gave an anxious thump at the sight.

"You can't do this," she pleaded, stepping closer.

"Why not?" Mell pulled a gun from the pile, giving the barrel a quick spin.

"Because someone will get *hurt*."

Mell gave her an incredulous look. "My sister is going to *die*."

"And Elsie? And Vera? And Ruth? Aren't they your family too?"

"They know what they're doing," Mell said, turning back to the weapons.

"Mell, please." Penelope fell to her knees next to the captain. "You can't possibly think that you're going to break Corinna out of jail without one of you getting hurt." She swallowed hard. "Getting killed."

She'd been so worried about preventing violence from coming to Fortuna that she had never thought about the gang getting hurt. But now it was all she could think about. Somewhere in the back of her mind, she knew that some faceless jailers would probably suffer at the hands of the gang, but it was Elsie's young face, Ruth's trusting smile, Vera's wary eyes that floated before her now. It was a suicide mission. If not for all of them, at least for some of them. No one broke out of jail just by storming the prison. Jail breaks, whether in books or the newspapers, were always carried out through cunning. Planning. Secrecy. Not the blunt force of what Mell intended.

Mell looked over at her, sadness in her dark eyes. "What else am I supposed to do?"

Penelope reached out to grip her arm. "Wait."

"Penelope, she's going to be executed in just over two days."

"So you have two days," Penelope insisted. "Wait for the deputy. It'll only take half an hour or so for the message to reach the sheriff, and for Deputy Greenman to get saddled up and ready. He'll be here within four hours."

Mell shook her head. "We could be in White Hills by then."

"Even if you managed, even if no one got hurt, Corinna would have to be on the run forever. Is that what you want for her?"

"If the only other choice is death?"

"But what if there is another choice?" Penelope said desperately, squeezing Mell's arm. "A third way, where no one gets hurt? If you say that Corinna didn't shoot that mayor, then Deputy Greenman *must* be lying. So get him to recant his story. Take him to the judge in White Hills and clear Corinna's name. Let her walk out of that jail as a free woman, not a fugitive."

"If he perjured himself once, why would he change his tune now?"

"Because he's a yellow-bellied coward who wouldn't holler at a fly," Penelope said in exasperation. "And you're *the* Mirage Currier."

It startled a laugh out of Mell. She looked back down at the weapons. Pistols, revolvers, bayonets, throwing stars, hunting knives. A hundred different ways to kill glittered in the electric lights of the room.

"I don't want anyone to die," she said quietly.

"Then wait. Just a few hours. If it doesn't work, if Greenman won't talk, then you'll still be in White Hills by midnight. You'll still have time. Trust me."

Mell was silent for a long, tense moment. Then her shoulders sagged. "Okay."

"Thank you." Penelope breathed in relief.

XIII.

Mell peered through her spyglass while the crew waited with bated breath. They were on deck, pressed to the floor-to-ceiling window, necks craned to watch the road that wound ponderously from Fortuna to Copper Creek. It had been over four hours since Penelope sent the telegram to Fortuna. The shadows were lengthening on the ground below them as the day ticked away. Everyone was restless except for Mell, who stood stock-still at the window, glass to her eye, barely breathing as she did what she'd promised Penelope. She waited.

Beside her, Penelope fidgeted, forcing herself to trust that she had done the right thing.

To trust that Lewis would talk.

"Wait."

The crew turned as one, heads whipping eagerly toward Mell.

"What?" Vera pressed closer.

Penelope squinted against the sun hanging low in the sky.

"Dust on the road," Mell said, her voice even. "I can't quite ... No, it is. It's horses."

"Horses," Penelope asked, startled. "Plural?"

Mell slowly lowered the glass, her expression unchanging. "Yes. There are at least five riders."

"Shit," Vera cursed, stomping her feet.

Penelope was stunned. For some reason, it hadn't occurred to her that Lewis wouldn't do what she told him to. He always had, in the past.

"Can I see?"

Wordlessly Mell handed over the glass. Penelope raised it to her eye, and noticed that her hands were shaking. Squinting, she peered through.

At first all she could see was red. A cumulus of red billowed up from the road, obscuring everything else. But after a moment she could make out shapes within the dust. Her heart sank as she counted the outlines of men. Five. No, six.

The *Star* was outnumbered.

She looked closer and her heart sank further. It was impossible to see the men's faces, but Penelope would know the shape of Wiley Barnett anywhere. Arrogance was written in every line of his body.

"It's the sheriff," she whispered, her throat gone dry.

Vera swore again, kicking useless at the floorboards. Mell remained eerily calm. She turned to Penelope.

"I know you didn't want anyone to get hurt. But it was always going to come to this," she said, almost flatly. Resigned.

"What?"

"Me and Barnett. He's been gunning for me for years." She spun to face her crew. Taking a deep breath, she barked, "Everyone, to arms!"

The crew sprang into action, running off in every direction. A flurry of activity spun around Penelope, but she remained rooted to the spot, unable to move.

She should have known Wiley would come for her. She was his property, after all.

Like Mell said, it was always going to come to this. Her and Wiley.

Penelope turned back to the window, pressing her forehead against the glass, hot from the blazing desert sun. The dust cloud that marked out Wiley's progress moved inexorably toward them down the only road in and out of town.

There was going to be a fight. She could hear the rattle of the barrel of a revolver, the click of a shotgun ready to fire, the soft *shing* of knives being sharpened. They would fight, and people would die.

Penelope stifled a sob, pressing her lips tightly together.

Soon, Wiley was close enough to see without the spyglass, the dot on the horizon focusing into the man she knew, the man she was destined for. Despite the distance to the ground, Penelope was sure she could make out the arrogance on his face.

"Six of them, Captain!"

The voice made Penelope start, turning to see Byrdie at the helm, the glass at her eye.

"We can take six," Mell said calmly, stepping up beside her steersman. Penelope's stomach turned.

For a second, time seemed to stand still, as every member of the crew held herself ready, waiting. Penelope expected to hear the sound of a shot being fired any second.

"Attention!" Wiley's voice blared out of an electric megaphone. The crew froze, ears perked. "This is a warning from the elected sheriff of Fortuna, Arizona Territory."

It felt far longer than twenty-four hours since Penelope had last heard that commanding tone. Her stomach swooped. Once again, she was caught off guard. She hadn't expected Wiley to *negotiate*. Realizing the danger, she spun helplessly toward Mell.

"You are to release Penelope Moser immediately." Feeling like she was choking, Penelope squeezed her eyes shut against the inevitable. "If you return my fiancée to me, we will not engage. I repeat, we will not engage."

It was like all sound ceased except for those words—*my fiancée*—reverberating through the cabin.

"What?" It was Ruth who spoke first, not a cry of disbelief or betrayal, but simple confusion.

They all looked at her, shocked. Anger tore across Vera's pretty face, crumpling it into something ugly. But it was Mell's face that hurt the most. Betrayal shone so fiercely in her dark eyes that Penelope had to turn her face away.

"I—"

"Is it true?" It wasn't Mell, or Vera, or even Ruth who spoke. It was cute little Byrdie, anger flashing across her face.

Penelope dropped her eyes to her feet. Corinna's dress looked wrong on her.

"Yes."

"I told you we shouldn't trust her!" Vera broke out explosively.

"Vera—"

"We should kill her now, teach that lying sonnabitch a lesson."

"Vera." June's voice cracked through the room like a bullet. She laid a hand on Vera's shoulder, steadying her.

Wiley's voice intruded again, booming imperiously through the room. "Release my fiancée to me, and I will not engage."

It was the most sincere he had ever sounded about her, and Penelope didn't believe a word of it.

"I don't..." she started desperately, not knowing who to address it to. Elsie, who knew she didn't love Wiley. Vera, who knew that men lied more than anyone else. Mell, who might feel more for her than the man on the ground.

Mell wrenched a megaphone from the corner of the deck and raised it to her lips.

"The hostage will be returned to you. Take her and promise to fire no shots."

Penelope closed her eyes.

"I promise," Wiley's voice boomed back.

"I'm sorry," Penelope whispered, her words lost in the sudden activity on the deck.

Ruth grabbed her arm, hauling her to the hatch.

"I'm sorry," Penelope said more fiercely, but Ruth just turned away.

It wasn't the coach they led her to. Ruth moved around her, businesslike, hooking her up to a harness.

"Here."

Byrdie held out Penelope's dirty clothes. She didn't know how Byrdie had produced them so quickly.

"Please," she said.

A frown settled over Byrdie's lips, making her look even younger than she was.

Penelope didn't begrudge them their anger. But she still knew something they didn't.

"Mell! I need to tell you something!"

"Save it," Vera snapped.

But Mell turned, meeting Penelope's eyes. "Congratulations, little librarian." For the first time, the pet name came out sounding mean. "You won. You and your *fiancé*."

"Mell, I—"

"Was this all part of your plan? You distract us while he gets the appeal thrown out? Is that why you kissed me?"

Penelope's jaw dropped. "*You* kissed *me*," she said. "And kidnapped me! I didn't ask for you to bring me here!"

"And I wish we never had. We might already have Corinna out and safe if it weren't for you."

The words were like a slap to the face. But Penelope knew they weren't true. The crew might never believe her, but she knew that overturning the sentence was still the best way to free Corinna.

"Lewis Greenman was never in White Hills." The words burst out of Penelope, drawing every eye on deck. "Not during the ambush. I don't know why, but Wiley made him lie at the trial."

"Don't listen to her. It's just another trick," Vera said.

"I have proof!" Penelope insisted. "I'm sorry I didn't tell you before. I found proof before you brought me here. I hid it in Fortuna." The words pushed out of Penelope in a rush. "I went looking for the evidence before I ever met you. I knew something wasn't right."

"You want me to believe that a woman willingly marrying *that man*—" Mell gestured below them, disgust on her face "—a woman who wants to be Mrs. Sheriff Barnett is on *our* side?"

"Who said I want that?" Penelope burst out explosively. "No one's *ever* asked me what I wanted." She paused, tears welling in her eyes. "Until I came here. Until I met you. All of you."

Mell hesitated.

"No one ever told me I had a choice," Penelope said firmly, holding back her tears. "But now I know. So I'm making a choice. Follow me to Fortuna. Meet me at the post office. I can give you the evidence you need. I don't know if it will free Corinna, but it undermines Lewis's testimony."

"How do I know this isn't another ploy? Another way to delay me? To keep me out of White Hills?"

"You don't. You barely know me. I barely know you. But I still know you all are a thousand times better than that man on the ground. I want to help you if you'll just let me."

Mell looked torn. "I—"

Somewhere a lever was thrown and the hatch below her feet opened. Penelope gave a shout as the floor gave way. With desperate hands she reached for Mell, her fingers slipping uselessly over the material of the captain's shirt. Out of the corner of her eye, she saw Vera pushing Ruth away from the crank that would lower Penelope to her fate. She dropped another foot, away from Mell. "Please. Follow me," she cried.

Wiley's voice cut across them. "Return my fiancée!"

"I'm more than his fiancée," Penelope said desperately, but her words were lost in the air swirling around her. With another lurch, she began to lower, down toward Wiley and the life she had always known.

XIV.

Wind whistled around Penelope as she was lowered, haltingly, to the ground. The land seemed to buck and sway beneath her as the ropes twisted and twirled. Her stomach crawled up her throat and squatted, miserably, at the back of her tongue. She didn't know what made her feel sicker: the dizzying descent or the fate that awaited.

Wiley and his posse were poised beneath her, hands resting on the hilts of their guns. They watched her with unreadable expressions as she was dangled down like a worm on a hook.

The ground rose up to meet her, and Penelope wondered for the first time how gentle a landing it would be, with Vera at the controls. She needn't have worried. Before she hit the desert sand, she came to a stop, dangling a foot off the ground, swaying gently.

Wiley slid from his horse. "Penelope."

She met his eyes. "Would you mind getting me down?"

He frowned; Penelope didn't know if he was expecting hysterics or bubbling gratitude, but she was tired of trying to meet other people's expectations. Sucking back the tears that had threatened to fall on board the *Star*, she decided that Wiley didn't get to have any of her emotions. He stepped forward, his large, rough hands fumbling with the buckles on the harness, closer and more intimate than they had ever been. She bit her lip and looked to the heavens, where the *Star* hovered over them. In a moment she was free, dropping from the harness with a grunt into Wiley's waiting arms.

He caught her like he expected her to always fall right into his grasp. She struggled free, smoothing down her dress.

"Are you all right?" he demanded.

"I'm fine."

"They didn't hurt you?"

"No. They were perfectly civil."

One of the men snorted unkindly.

"They took you hostage," Wiley snapped.

"They were hoping to negotiate." She pointedly looked around her. "Where's Lewis?"

"Back at the station where he belongs," Wiley snapped. "What did they want with him anyway?"

Penelope wondered if the crew was watching from the deck, Penelope and Wiley framed in the round lens of the spyglass. She took a small step away from him.

"To talk to him, I imagine. That's what they said in the telegram."

"They didn't tell you anything else?" Wiley closed the gap between them again, looming above her, making use of his height.

Penelope met his gaze, keeping her face blank. "Why would they? I was just a hostage."

"You said they treated you well."

"They did. But they didn't exactly bring me into their inner circle."

"No, of course not." Wiley turned away. "You're just a way to get to me."

"Can we go home now?" Penelope asked. "I want to see my father."

"Of course. He wanted to come."

But he hadn't. How hard had her father really lobbied to come on such a dangerous mission?

"You'll ride with me," Wiley barked, returning to his horse.

"What about the *Star*?" Mace growled. "We just gonna let the bitches go?"

Wiley shot him a fierce look. "We came for my fiancée. We need to make sure Miss Moser gets home safe and sound."

"But—"

"A civilian's safety is our first priority, is that clear?"

Mace subsided sulkily.

With a rough grip around her waist, Wiley lifted Penelope up onto the back of his fiery stallion. The horse pawed the ground, snorting. Wiley swung up behind her, pressing against the length of her in the saddle. "Sorry we don't got no lady's saddle," he said into her ear, his breath gusting roughly over her. "We weren't sure we were gonna get you back."

"I can ride astride."

"I'll bet she can," Seth Byrne snickered, drawing a burst of laughter from the other men. Penelope stiffened.

Wiley didn't chide them, just set his spurs into the horse and turned for home. Penelope looked up one last time, the silhouette of the *Star* against the bright sky burning into her mind.

They galloped back to Fortuna.

Ashes made a fuss. Penelope had known he would. He was waiting on the steps of the sheriff's station, wringing his hands, when they rode up. Penelope didn't doubt he'd been pacing and sniffing into a fine chambray handkerchief since Wiley left Fortuna.

He pulled her into a tight embrace, gushing over the danger she had faced and how terrified he had been. Penelope patted him on the back, making soothing noises like he was a startled animal.

Townspeople had gathered, clucking over her misfortune, repeating over and over again how close to death she had come. She was passed from Ashes into the hands of the women of the town, spun through the arms of Charlotte Storey, Elizabeth Mycock, Cathryn Houser, and the rest.

"You must have been so frightened!" they cooed at her.

Penelope smiled and nodded and said how glad she was to be home. Yes, it was such a close call; yes, she was lucky to be alive; yes, she had thanked Wiley for going all that way to save her.

Finally her father came to her rescue. "It's late. I'm sure Penelope wants to get home and get some rest," he called out over the crowd, fishing her back out from the throng.

She waved halfheartedly to the sea of well-wishers and the morbidly curious and let her father steer her away.

Wiley trotted after them.

"Everything all right with the *Star*?" Ashes asked the sheriff over Penelope's head.

"Didn't get much engagement. They caved immediately, as I knew they would. Buncha chickenshits."

"Language!" Ashes tutted, but he looked pleased nonetheless. "What's your plan now?"

"Still got eyes on them in Copper Creek. I reckon they're going to try something, what with the little one set to dangle on Monday morning." A cruel gleam came into his eyes. "And when they do, well," he smiled. "I've got more than 'a bunch of lowlifes and criminals' to back me up now."

Penelope blanched to hear her own words flung back at her. "What do you mean?"

Wiley shot her a gloating smile. "The townsfolk were real upset to hear you'd been snatched up. If Mirage Currier could get you, she could get any of their wives or daughters."

It was strange to hear the name *Mirage* now; Mell was nothing but a flesh-and-blood woman, smaller than anyone ever expected, soft and hard in turns, and so much more than an illusion or a criminal mastermind.

"God only knows what she'd do with a pretty young thing once she had her."

"I told you—" Penelope bristled, but Wiley spoke over her.

"Men are lining up to fight the scourge of the *Star* with me now. When Mirage Currier makes a move and I need an army, I've got one. I guess I got you to thank for that."

Penelope's heart sank and she asked weakly, "How many?"

"Twenty some good men, at minimum."

The *Persephone Star* might be able to take six, but they'd never best twenty, especially not on unfamiliar ground.

Penelope took a deep breath, her resolve hardening. She had to get the papers out of the sheriff's office and get them to Mell before Wiley could start a war.

How hard could it be?

She let the men steer her back home, into the familiar surroundings. Sarah was practically weeping as she met them at the door and had to be roughly shooed away by Wiley as Ashes herded Penelope toward her bedroom.

"Now, you get right to bed. You must be exhausted." He hesitated, then drew her into a tight hug, their first in years. "I'm so glad to have you home safe, little girl," he muttered into her hair.

Penelope hugged back, surprised by how much she needed it. "Thanks, Daddy. Sorry to worry you."

"No need for you to apologize!" Ashes tutted, drawing back and smoothing her hair away from her face. "You were very brave."

She thought that was true, but not in the way Ashes meant, and not in a way he'd approve of. The feel of Mell's mouth against her own rushed into her mind, and her cheeks heated.

"Now, straight to bed," Ashes reminded her, wagging his meaty finger. She gave him a reassuring smile and let him close her into the dim interior of her room.

Penelope sat down on the edge of her bed, her mind racing. Would Mell believe her? Would she come for the papers?

Whether she did or not, Penelope knew she had to get that evidence. She would take it to White Hills herself if she had to. But how was she supposed to get into Wiley's office when every man in Fortuna was in the sheriff's station, arming themselves for battle, and her father was just outside her door?

Penelope lay back with an anguished groan. She felt more trapped in her own bedroom than she ever had on board the *Star*.

There was no clock in her room, but the summer sun had already set, washing the desert in cool indigos, so she knew it had to be ten o'clock or later. Her father would go to bed soon, but what about the men at the sheriff's station? Would they stay up all night, their eyes on the sky? Penelope resolved to deal with that when the time came. First, she had to get out of the house. She would wait until everyone was in bed and everything was quiet, and then she would slip out of the house as silently as she could.

For the moment, all she could do was wait.

A noise startled Penelope out of sleep. She sat up in bed, clutching her sheets to her chest a second too late as people burst into her room.

A noise of distress escaped her throat, and she cowered back against the bedframe before her father's voice boomed through the room to reassure her.

Ashes stood in the doorway with Lewis Greenman ducking into his shadow.

"What are you doing?" Penelope demanded, her voice little more than a screech.

"The *Star* is on the move, miss," Lewis stammered, turning his face away from the sight of her in bed.

"Wh—where to?" Penelope asked, heart in her throat.

"They're headed right for us." Lewis's face was grim, and Penelope had to fight to match his expression when all she wanted to do was smile. Mell had listened to her, had *believed* her.

"Sheriff in Copper Creek says we only got an hour," Lewis continued.

There was no clock in Penelope's bedroom, though it was still dark outside her curtains. She didn't know how long she'd slept, how long she'd wasted. She had insisted Mell come for her, and now she was caught, still half-asleep and without the papers.

"Well, you better get down to the station, then, hadn't you?" she suggested, trying to calculate the time. If Wiley was waiting for Lewis, she'd have to hang back by at least twenty minutes before heading into town, counting on being met by an empty station while Wiley rallied his army of farmers, layabouts, and clerks.

That would give her just enough time to get into the station, retrieve the papers, and get to a location where she could meet the *Star*—hopefully without any shots being fired.

Penelope slid a guilty look at her father. He would be devastated when Mell got the papers to White Hills and Wiley's lies were revealed. It would reflect badly on him as the self-styled patriarch of Fortuna.

Or worse yet, he would stick by Wiley and believe whatever lies the sheriff fed him. Either way, the end of Penelope's engagement to the sheriff would hurt Ashes and would hurt her relationship with him. Perhaps irrevocably.

But if Corinna died, it would break Mell beyond recognition.

Lewis interrupted her train of thought. "Not me, ma'am."

Penelope looked at him sharply. "What?"

He scuffed his shoes against the floor. "Wiley don't want me in this fight."

Penelope frowned. It didn't matter to her whether Lewis was at Wiley's side or not, but his presence in her bedroom suddenly seemed more than suspicious. If he'd been sent to protect her, then there was no chance of slipping away.

"Why, Lewis Greenman!" She gasped pointedly. "You're the deputy, aren't you? Your place is at the sheriff's side."

Blotchy patches of red broke out over Lewis's cheeks. "I'm not shirking duty, ma'am," he mumbled at his shoes.

"Of course not!" Ashes leapt in, slapping the poor deputy heartily on the shoulder. "Lewis is here to protect you."

"But Wiley will need every man, won't he?"

"Those bandits wanted Lewis for something," Ashes reminded her, his voice full of foreboding. "It's best for the whole town if he steers right clear of them."

Lewis relaxed under Ashes's approbation. "That's right, Miss Moser. Wiley don't want me getting caught up in whatever their plot is." He looked up, meeting her eyes earnestly. "And you neither."

Penelope was still turning over ways to slip away and get to the sheriff's stations when Lewis's next words stopped her in her tracks.

"He's got us tickets on the five fifteen out of town."

Her head jerked up. "Excuse me?"

"Oh, I know it's sudden," Ashes placated, stepping forward to drape a fatherly arm over her shoulder. "But you've got time to get a bag together and get yourself presentable, don't worry."

"But—" Penelope shook her head, trying to make sense of their words. "Where am I meant to be going?"

"Why, to Yuma, of course."

The name of the city tripped horribly in Penelope's brain. It was the main hub for coaches and steamboats in the Arizona territory, a booming metropolis compared to most of the outposts. If Wiley sent her to Yuma, he could send her on to anywhere. Out of the territory, out of the West. With her father's permission, he could put her on a coach without even telling her where she was going. No one would question it.

"What on earth for?"

Ashes and Lewis turned identical frowns on her.

"To protect you," her father said sternly. "You were kidnapped once, remember?"

"I could hardly forget," Penelope snapped. Had it only been the day before that she was with the crew on the *Star*, meeting June's warm gaze, Byrdie's mischievous smile, or the spark that twinkled in Mell's eyes?

Now—faced with the twin concern of her father and Lewis, men of different ages, statures, and backgrounds, but united in their assurance that they knew better than she did—it seemed impossible.

She wrapped her arms around herself, a shield against the world, and tried to sound reasonable. "I can't go to Yuma. It's ridiculous. I've only just got home."

Ashes tutted. "I *know*, darling. But that's the very reason you must go. Those ruffians know who you are now. They know you're close to Wiley. You're close to me. They've already tried to use you to get to the important men in this town."

Men. It was always about the men. Even when it was about her, it wasn't.

"So I'm to be sent away from my home and my family? My job?"

"You won't be gone for long," Ashes said, steering steered her gently toward her wardrobe. "Just until Wiley sorts out this nasty business. After all, he wouldn't want to delay the wedding." He gave her an indulgent smile.

Penelope fought the urge to recoil, knowing what Wiley's version of "sorting out" the business would consist of. He wouldn't be happy until every last person on the *Star* was dead, even middle-aged June who had never lifted a weapon in her life. He had a secret to hide, after all.

A secret that only Penelope could reveal; if she could only get away from the helpful men around her.

"I'll sit with you while you pack a bag," Ashes offered genially. "And Lewis will wait downstairs, in case Wiley sends news."

"But . . . Father," Penelope said desperately. "I don't want to go."

"Now, now." Ashes gave her another nudge to start packing. "I know you're a capable young woman, but are you going to deny that your father knows best? Or your fiancé?"

There was no way to argue.

Penelope began shoving things into a small carry-bag while Lewis retreated down the stairs. She didn't know how she was supposed to get away now, not with the paternalism of her father and Wiley bearing down upon her.

She only needed a few minutes in the sheriff's station, but it seemed she wouldn't be left alone for a second.

"Oh no," she said, forcing distress into her voice. "I've left my favorite books at the office."

Ashes laughed.

"I can't possibly travel without them," Penelope coaxed. "I'm in the middle of a novel!"

"I think you can wait until there aren't lives on the line to find out how it ends," Ashes said gently.

"But who knows how long I'll be gone!"

Ashes looked at her seriously. "There are books in Yuma. I need to know my precious little girl is safe." He laid a meaty hand on her shoulder. "You're all I have left, Penny."

He hadn't called her that since she was a little girl, when her mother died. Penelope wilted under the weight of the endearment.

"Come on, now," he said. "You don't want to miss your train."

"No, Daddy," she agreed dully.

She just didn't know how to be a disappointment to her father, the only family she'd had for so long. Not even when the betrayal that had blazed in Mell's eyes was still burned into her retinas. She let herself be steered through the motions of preparing for her trip to Yuma.

 # XV.

The train chugged sluggishly into view, a cloud of steam enveloping the sparse station that marked out Fortuna on the line. Penelope sat next to Lewis, her bag at her feet, a ticket clutched in her hands. Her knuckles were white with how tight she was holding it. Every time she closed her eyes, Mell's face swam into view, betrayal burning in her eyes. If only she hadn't fallen asleep. If only she had told Mell about the papers earlier. It would be Penelope's fault now if Corinna was executed.

The conductor hopped onto the platform as the train slowed to a halt, his feet hitting wood before the engine even stopped. "Fortuna!" His voice carried down the line. "All off for Fortuna!"

A single man struggled off the train, looking too naïve for the hardships that might await him in the small town. Penelope watched him go, his movements flustered and unsure, wishing that she could do anything to change places with him, to be heading away from the steaming machinery instead of into it.

"Come on, miss," Lewis said, standing resolutely. "The train don't linger long in a backwoods station like ours."

Penelope rose wordlessly beside him. It had been nearly an hour since Lewis burst into her bedroom. The *Star* must be almost upon Fortuna, Wiley's army poised to meet it. A lump rose in her throat, and she swallowed insistently, trying to choke it back down.

"Let me take that bag for you, ma'am," the conductor said gallantly, sweeping the small case out of Penelope's grip. Lewis stepped up into the waiting train as the conductor held out a hand for Penelope to do the same. She faltered, her head turning toward town.

"First time on a train?" the conductor asked indulgently. "Safe as can be, don't worry."

"It's not my safety I'm worried about," she muttered, hauling herself up into the train of her own accord.

She followed Lewis through the dim interior of the first-class carriage. Ashes had spared no expense for his little girl.

She dropped onto a plush seat with a sigh. Lewis sat down at the nearby table, shooting nervous glances her way. Penelope gazed out the window, straining her eyes toward the horizon. Was that a dark shape in the sky? A small sound caught her ear and she started— Was that gunfire? Had it already begun?

The cowardice of sitting in that ridiculous luxury while people were dying rose up her throat like bile.

No. She refused to be a good girl who did what she was told any longer. Mell had come to Fortuna because Penelope had asked her to. And Penelope was not going to let her down.

"Lewis."

"Ma'am?"

"Why is Wiley sending you away?"

"Well, I told you. He's worried—"

Penelope cut him off, turning sharply on him. "Why is he *really* sending you away? Is it because you weren't in White Hills the day of the gunfight?"

Lewis's eyes widened. "What?"

Penelope stood abruptly, looming over him. "I know you were here in Fortuna that day, Lewis. I know you lied to that judge."

He shrank back in his seat. "How? Did Wiley say...?" He shook his head. "He said no one could know!"

Penelope leaned over him. "Why did he say that, Lewis? Is it because Corinna Currier didn't shoot Mayor Bailey?"

"It's not like Wiley meant to hit him, miss. You have to know that!" The words burst out of the lean deputy.

Penelope staggered a step back. "*Wiley* shot him?"

"It was an accident, but it could have ruined his career," Lewis continued insistently. "Imagine where Fortuna would be without him!"

"So you two decided to sacrifice a *young girl* to save Wiley's career?"

Lewis frowned, faltering. "She's just a criminal."

"She's a *child*, and she never shot anyone." Penelope straightened. "Lewis Greenman, I hope the shame of this keeps you awake every night for the rest of your miserable life." She turned away from him.

"Where are you going?"

"Last call for Fortuna!" the conductor's voice sang down the platform. A gust of steam billowed outside the windows.

"Wait!" Penelope yelled. "I'm getting off!"

"Miss Moser!" Lewis shot up out of his seat.

She raced to the door of the carriage and flung it open. The conductor was nowhere to be seen. The train gave a long whistle, and Penelope hurled herself out the door just as the engine began chugging.

"Miss Moser!"

She stumbled onto the platform, her ankle turning slightly at the drop from the train. She glanced over her shoulder to see Lewis hanging out the carriage door, his shouts lost under the deafening noise of the train steaming out of the station.

Penelope looked around anxiously. There were no other people on the platform, and Lewis wouldn't be able to get a message to Wiley until the next station. She had time if she hurried.

Penelope gathered up her long skirts, wishing she'd given more thought to Mell's offer of trousers, and broke into a run.

As she left the station, the *Star* came into view, hovering above Main Street. Solid and heavy in the sky.

Even in the early morning the desert sun was hot, and Penelope wasn't used to doing more than ambling the distance between her house and the post office. "Ladies" were supposed to sneer at the ranchers' wives who did physical labor, herding cattle and working long hours in the field.

Now Penelope scoffed. A woman should be able to run if she needed to.

The muggy air scraped her throat and lungs as her feet kicked up dust on the road into town. She couldn't hear anything yet, didn't know how long the *Star* had been docked in Fortuna.

She didn't know if she was already too late.

The town was eerily quiet as Penelope sped onto Main Street. The shops were shut and the houses had their doors and shutters pulled firmly closed. No one seemed to be stirring.

She couldn't see anyone bleeding, so she had to believe there was still time.

Penelope swept her sweaty curls off her face and headed for the sheriff's station. It was dark when she arrived. The door hung open, ominous.

Warily, she approached. Inside, evidence of the coming fight was everywhere: the station lay in disarray; the armory was open and empty. Quickly Penelope picked her way through the items knocked to the floor in the men's hurry.

She held her breath as she reached the hiding place, sending up a prayer to the heavens. There was no reason for anyone to go rifling through these boxes, but her heart was in her throat as she reached in, fingers groping for the evidence that could save Corinna Currier.

Paper rustled under Penelope's hand, and she sighed in relief as she drew out the telegraph receipt and letter.

They wouldn't prove that Wiley had shot Mayor Bailey, but she hoped they'd be enough to clear Corinna's name.

She hadn't had time to consider the weight of Lewis's confession. All she knew was Wiley's guilt had propelled her off the train. To lie to a judge was bad enough, but to shoot a man and blame it on a girl was monstrous. She recoiled at the knowledge that the man responsible was still her fiancé; she was still pledged to him for life.

Though she had a feeling that after today he wouldn't want her anymore.

Penelope tucked the papers resolutely into her pocket and turned toward the door.

A shot rang out, a sharp *crack* that shattered the silence of town.

Penelope faltered. The soft morning light filtered in through the open door, catching on something under a pile of hastily pushed-aside papers, making it glimmer. She put her hand on the gun, feeling its shape under her palm.

Without allowing herself to think, she picked it up and tucked it into the waistband of her skirt, before striding out of the office, onto the deserted street.

It went against her every instinct to walk toward the sound of the gunshot, but she had to find Mell before Wiley did.

The street was emptier than she had ever seen it. Where were Wiley's men? Were they watching her? Penelope cast her eyes over the buildings, wondering whether a weapon was pointed at her through the slats of every shutter she walked past.

An aborted shout cut through the thick air, and Penelope turned her head sharply. It had come from near the post office. She sped up, trotting down the road, trying to be alert enough to dive for cover if necessary.

She'd never been in a gunfight. She didn't quite know what to do.

The street was still quiet, but something in the air seemed to be stirring. Penelope stopped in front of the post office, her breath catching at the sight of the open door. Someone was inside.

Penelope crept forward, pressing close to the wall of the building. The person inside might be trigger happy, and it wouldn't do anyone any good if she got shot. Craning her neck, she peered around the open door, squinting into the dimly lit interior.

At first, she couldn't make anything out. It was just the same familiar room in which she'd spent the last year: her orderly pencils, her shining telegraph machine, her sad little shelf of books. She hesitated, one hand on the doorframe.

A soft noise caught her ear. She froze, straining her eyes in the low light. A figure hunched behind the tall counter, poised by the back window. It was unmistakably Wiley: the tension of his shoulders, the steadiness of his hands as he leveled his gun. Penelope drew back, trying not to make a sound.

If she left now, he'd never know she had been there. She still had time to find one of the *Star*'s crew and get them the papers. She took a hesitant step back, her eyes never leaving the sheriff.

Movement out the back window made him tense, his finger twitching on the trigger of his gun.

Penelope stopped, leaning forward to make out the scene framed by her office window.

Mell was creeping carefully out from behind the barrels stacked beside the general store. She was bent close to the ground, gun in hand, but Wiley had his rifle trained right on her. He leaned forward slightly, eyes narrowing behind the sight.

Penelope didn't think. The gun was in her hand in a second, warm from where it had been pressed against her skin.

Mell's head came up at the crack of the shot, and their eyes met through the window.

Wiley let out a hoarse shout, rolling back toward the room, shifting his rifle on his shoulder and training it on his assailant. Blood blossomed under his shirt, pumping sluggishly from the flesh wound in his side.

Suddenly everything was happening at once. Wiley's eyes widened and the gun slackened in his grip. "You?" he croaked, just as Mell screamed, "Run!" Her voice reverberated through the silence of the street.

At the sound, shots fired, the sharp cracking of several guns. Penelope heard shouting, picking out Vera's voice, then Mace's and Seth's.

She couldn't move, frozen with her gaze locked on Wiley.

His head lolled down to take in the blood seeping through his shirt with a look of disbelief. "Why the hell did you shoot me?"

"I know you shot Mayor Bailey."

Wiley's head jerked up, but anger quickly replaced surprise. "So?" he snarled, tightening his grip on his rifle.

Penelope braced herself, raising her gun once again. "You're not going to get away with this." Her finger pressed tight on the trigger, just waiting for him to move.

Confusion clouded Wiley's eyes. "You're my fiancée." He slid down the wall to the floor, rifle falling to his side as he groped at his wound.

Penelope gritted her teeth and steadied the gun.

"Goddamn it, little librarian!" Mell skidded into the post office. "I said to *run*."

She was flushed, breathless, eyes bright with panic. A streak of dirt smeared across her upturned nose, and disheveled hair spilled into her eyes. She was the most beautiful thing Penelope had ever seen.

"You came," she said, unable to restrain her smile.

"I came." Mell's eyes widened as she took in the scene in the post office: the gun in Penelope's hands, and the blood seeping through

Wiley's shirt. "Did you ... did you *shoot* him?" She gasped. "I thought you were going to *marry* him."

"He was going to shoot you," Penelope said.

It was that simple. The universe had asked her to make a choice, and she'd made it. It had been a split-second decision, but Penelope didn't regret it. She would choose Mell every time.

"Oh." Mell looked stunned, then slightly hopeful.

"You're working with *those whores*?" Wiley gasped, his eyes darting between them.

"They're not whores," Penelope spat, her eyes back on the sheriff.

"They're criminals."

Penelope steadied her gun. "So are you. I have evidence to prove what you've done. We're going to take it to White Hills and give it to the judge."

"So what, you're going to run off on the *Star*? Become some kind of lady Robin Hood?"

"You *knew*," Penelope snarled. "You knew they were doing good all along."

Wiley snorted, clamping a hand over his wound immediately after as fresh blood bubbled up. "I'm the one doing good around here, you bitch. I'm the law."

"You don't care about the law." Penelope said. "You just like the power."

"You wanna run around playing at saving the world and letting a woman try to do a man's job between your legs, then be my guest." Wiley raised a meaty finger, his skin stained red with his own blood. "But you better keep an eye over your shoulder, because I'm going to be right on your tails. Every step of the way."

"The only place you're going to be is in jail," Penelope said.

"For lying on the stand?" Mell whispered incredulously.

"For shooting Mayor Bailey and framing Corinna."

"What? You son of a bitch!" Mell lunged forward, but Penelope caught her by the arm.

"Oh, the little girl's got some bite after all," Wiley sneered.

"She's a woman," Penelope insisted. "And so am I. And we don't need to stoop to your level. We'll see you at your sentencing."

Mell turned, meeting her eyes. She was clearly livid, but she took a deep, steadying breath. "You have the evidence?"

Penelope nodded. "Just about. Here." She held the gun out to Mell. "You're better with this than I am."

"I don't know," Mell said, her eyes on Wiley. "You did a pretty good job." But she took the gun, keeping it steady on the sheriff as Penelope leaned across the old familiar counter of the post office. Postmaster Gillespie's files from the last two years were there, neatly organized and stored by Penelope soon after she took over the job. She grabbed them. No point leaving anything behind.

"Okay. I'm ready."

Mell met her eyes. "I had a speech planned about how you should come with us. But"—she tipped her head at Wiley's bleeding form—"I guess you don't have much choice now."

Penelope's heart buoyed; she'd been afraid she wouldn't be welcomed back on the *Star*. "I had a choice," she assured Mell, "and I made it."

Mell's answering smile lit up her face.

Wiley looked between them with disgust. "This can't be what you want."

Penelope barely spared him a glance. "Tell my father I love him, all right? It's the least you can do."

"I would have given you a good life," he protested.

Penelope fixed him with a cold stare. "Not the life I wanted." She turned to Mell. "Let's go."

"Wait," Mell said. "Not without these."

She darted over to the far wall, sweeping the books off the small library shelf. An incredulous laugh escaped Penelope's throat.

"Are you crazy?"

"A librarian needs her books," Mell said with a grin. "Now come on, before his backup shows up." Mell nudged past her to the door. "Follow me, and keep your eyes open!"

She sprinted out into the street and, without a moment's hesitance over the life she was leaving behind, Penelope ran after her. Out in the street, she grabbed Mell's hand. Mell looked back, surprised, and Penelope tugged, reeling her in until she could catch Mell's mouth with her own. They were both breathless, panting and grimy, books pressed uncomfortably between them. It was perfect. *This*, thought Penelope. *This, this, this.*

"Librarian," Mell breathed into her mouth. "We're going to get shot."

It startled a laugh out of Penelope that Mell swallowed up in another kiss. Reluctantly she pulled away. Mell tipped her face like she wanted to chase Penelope's lips with her own.

A sound at the end of the deserted street made them both jump. "Run!" Penelope said, tangling their fingers together and pulling Mell after her.

"That's what I've been saying the whole time!" Mell said, sprinting after her. "Follow the *Star*!"

The ship shone in the morning light, glittering like a beacon to guide them home. As they ran toward it, the hatch opened and something like a crow's nest descended to scoop them up into safety.

XVI.

The cabin was in a state of chaos when Mell and Penelope struggled back on board the *Persephone Star*. The other women were there already, trying to recover from the standoff they'd faced on the ground. June was fretting over Vera, patting gently at some wounds even while Vera batted her away, crossly declaring that she was fine. Elsie, quite disheveled herself, was checking Ruth over, making the big woman stoop down while Elsie peered into her eyes, letting Penelope know that Ruth must have taken a wallop to the head. Byrdie was the only one absent; Penelope had to assume that she was at the wheel, ready to speed away when all the troops came home.

The hatch in the floor of the cabin slammed shut after them, the sound ricocheting around the big space. Four pairs of eyes whipped toward them.

Vera's usual scowl deepened, but June and Elsie looked cautiously optimistic. Ruth just seemed happy to see everyone on board and in one piece.

"What's *she* doing here?" Vera asked, crossing her arms tightly and sneering at Penelope like she was the dirt on her boots.

"Oh, shove it, Vera. She *shot* the *sheriff*," Mell panted, out of breath from their sprint and their climb.

"She *what*?" June gasped, a hand flying to her mouth.

"In the back!" Mell crowed.

"Now, it wasn't like that and you know it," Penelope said. "He was going to shoot you."

"Well, well." Vera's expression had cleared, something like respect in her eyes. "Is he dead?"

"No!" Penelope said, aghast.

"Still," Vera said, with a considering pout. "Maybe we'll make something of you, after all."

"*Vera*," June huffed, pushing to the fore. She took Penelope's arm with maternal care. "Are you all right?"

Penelope was pretty sure she shouldn't be. She'd shot a man—she'd shot her *fiancé*—and run off with a band of outlaws, with nothing but the books in her arms. But, actually: "I'm fine. I'm great, I think," she said, her cheeks heating. She could still taste Mell on her lips.

"*Oh*," Elsie said knowingly.

"But are you hurt?" June insisted.

It was like being enveloped in a warm blanket. June's worry was miles away from the fussing Ashes had done the previous day. She wasn't making a scene because it was expected; she was worried about Penelope.

Penelope slid a hand over June's, where it rested on her arm. "I'm all right. Mell was there to protect me."

"You didn't need it," Mell said, bumping shoulders jovially. "You're a regular gunslinger."

"I would really prefer to never shoot anyone ever again," Penelope said honestly. The way the bullet had ripped into Wiley, sending him staggering, was seared into her brain. She would see that image on the back of her eyelids for the rest of her life.

"Aw, that's all right," Ruth said. "June and Byrdie don't fight neither. But we still need them."

Penelope flashed her a smile. "Thank you, Ruth."

Ruth grinned. Penelope looked around at the circle of faces, realizing she felt like she belonged there. She felt like she was part of something. It was like the feeling working the telegraph had given her, but being part of the Line was anonymous and lonely work. She was a cog in a machine, and every cog spun in isolation. Here, she could be a part of something, something as important as the Line, but with company. Friends. She surreptitiously glanced at Mell, taking in the way she glowed with excitement at the outcome of the fight, her cheeks dewy and flushed, her eyes bright. Maybe even something else.

"So what now?" Vera asked. "We've got the librarian but no sheriff. Seems we're back where we started."

"Not exactly," Penelope said, pulling the papers out of her pocket. Everyone crowded close. "What is that?"

"Evidence," Penelope said with satisfaction.

June and Vera understood the fastest—they were both sharp as tacks. "Is it enough?" June asked, gaze flying hopefully to Mell.

"I hope so," Penelope breathed.

"It will be," Mell said, with all the overconfidence of a legendary outlaw. "It has to be. But first we have to get to White Hills."

"I'll tell Byrdie!" Elsie said, scampering away to the upper decks.

"No, wait!" June said. "We need the lawyer."

"There's no time!" Mell said. "He's three hundred miles away in Tucson."

"The judge isn't going to talk to you, Mell. You know that."

"So we'll make him," Vera growled, dropping her hand to the pistol that sat, glittering in the glow of the electric lights, in the holster strapped to her naked thigh.

"He'll listen," Penelope said firmly. She didn't want any violence. Not again. "He'll *have* to."

June didn't seem convinced, but the ship was already lurching into movement. Penelope swayed on her feet; for the rest, it was like the ship hadn't moved at all.

"You'll get your sea legs, don't worry," Mell said, grabbing her arm to steady her.

Vera arched an eyebrow at the way Mell held her. Heat rose to Penelope's cheeks, but she met Vera's gaze defiantly. People like Wiley might think there was something to be ashamed of in the way she felt about Mell, but Penelope didn't.

"So, you're staying, then?" Vera asked, but it wasn't mean.

"Yes." Penelope paused. "If you'll have me." She met each of the crew's gaze in turn. She didn't know how things worked on the ship, if Mell's word was simply law, but she was hoping to be welcomed by the whole crew.

June smiled. "Of course, dear."

"Another person on the rota means one fewer day that I have to swab the decks," Vera said with a careless shrug, but a small smile threatened to curl up her red lips.

Ruth's eyes were on the place where Mell's fingers loosely curled around Penelope's wrist. "Does this mean you're Mell's wife now?"

"Okay!" Vera said loudly. "Everyone up on deck. Lots to do to get ready." She began ushering Ruth from the room.

"What?" Ruth protested, as June followed, hiding her smile.

"Ruth didn't mean that," Mell said quickly, the second they were alone. "She just . . . you know, she thinks in black-and-white. When a man and woman court, they get married . . . but of course, we're two women. And you're going to be a *valuable* member of the crew outside of what we're . . ." Mell stumbled over her words.

"Mell," Penelope tried to interrupt.

"The ship could really use a library, for one. Ruth can't read, but I know she'd like to know how, and Elsie's not much better at it, so you'll be a real help to all of us."

"*Mell.*"

Mell slammed her lips shut, eyes wide. She didn't look a bit like Mirage Currier, famed outlaw, in that moment. She just looked like a young woman who was anxious and hopeful all at the same time, her emotions a tangled mess inside herself.

"I don't mind what Ruth says." Penelope reached out, twining their fingers together. "But let's see where things go before we start talking marriage."

Mell laughed, her cheeks pink, but still asked, "You know you don't have to, right? You're welcome here no matter what."

It was what neither Wiley nor her father had ever said. It was what she had longed to hear every day since the engagement was announced. "I *know*, Mell."

"Well, okay then." Mell ducked her head and then glanced up again, catching Penelope's gaze through the sweep of her lashes. It was . . . shy, almost. Again, a word Penelope never would have associated with the infamous Mirage Currier.

But this was just Mell, who stepped up to Penelope hesitantly. "I'm glad you're here, little librarian."

Penelope's cheeks warmed. "Me too," she whispered.

Mell tipped her head up and this time Penelope met her, brushing their lips together in a featherlight kiss. The contact sizzled through her. Emboldened, she fit her mouth over Mell's, kissing her like she had always wanted to be kissed: tenderly and sweetly.

"Thank you for following me," she said as she pulled back.

Mell blinked, looking almost stunned. Then she grinned. "Thanks for shooting that bastard and saving my life."

"*Mell*," Penelope groaned, putting her hands over her face.

Mell relented. "Come on. Vera was right. There's lots to do before we get to White Hills."

"Speaking of," Penelope said. "Can I use some paper and ink?"

XVII.

At nine o'clock on a Saturday morning, the busy town of White Hills was bustling. Homesteaders who'd been up with the sun unloaded their goods at the stores along the main street, calling out greetings to each other across the road that teemed with carts and horses. Women window-shopped, pausing to inspect the goods carefully laid out.

June had insisted that they dock out of town and take the carriage, in the hopes of attracting little notice in a town that would never wish them well—not after the shoot-out. Now the carriage bundled through the streets, puffing steam in its wake, and barely drawing a spare glance from the people outside.

They drove through the town, right past the impressive town hall, to the stately houses that sat on its edges. "If Judge McCoy isn't out of bed, then we'll get him out of bed," Mell said with a grim smile. Here, the wooden slats of the buildings were painted a showy white, and efforts had been made to landscape in the midst of the desert.

Vera and Ruth stayed in the carriage, ready for a quick getaway, as Mell and Penelope slipped out.

Mell kept her eyes on the road as Penelope knocked at the imposing door. After a moment, a girl's face peered out at them.

"Yes?" she asked. The smile on her face dropped as her eyes drifted behind Penelope to Mell.

"We need to speak to Judge McCoy," Penelope said firmly.

"I—" The girl faltered, her eyes never leaving Mell's trousers or her gun.

"It's a matter of some urgency," Penelope said.

"Judge McCoy don't do business on Saturdays," the girl said, edging the door closed. "You'll have to see him in his office on Monday."

"Afraid not, sweetheart," Mell said, stopping the door with her foot. "You see, by the time he's in his office on Monday, my sister will be dead."

"Mirage Currier," the girl squeaked, eyes wide. She tried desperately to slam the door shut.

The girl couldn't be more than fifteen, and she was no match for Mell. Mell shouldered her way in, pushing the girl aside.

"It's all right," Penelope whispered to the girl, who was shaking like a leaf. "You just go upstairs and do your work. Nothing's going to happen."

Sounds came from down the opulent corridor: the clink of silverware and dishes. "Come on," Mell hissed. She pulled her gun.

"Put that away!" Penelope said, hurrying after her. "We're here with legitimate evidence. We don't need to shoot anyone."

Mell frowned but slipped the revolver back into its holster.

In the dining room, the judge and his wife were eating breakfast.

His wife's fork clattered to her plate as Mell and Penelope stepped into the room.

The judge was on his feet in a second, clasping his dressing gown tight around him. "Thomas!" he barked.

"There is no need to be alarmed!" Penelope said, stepping forward hurriedly, before Mell could pull her weapon again. "We just want to talk to you."

"I've had her brand of talking before," Judge McCoy said. His wife trembled.

Penelope shot Mell a look. *What did you do?* she mouthed. Mell just shrugged, reaching out to grab a knife off the table. She twirled it in her fingers.

"I have evidence to present," Penelope said. "In the Corinna Currier case."

The judge's gaze tracked to her and he frowned. "And who are you?"

Penelope drew herself up. "I am the postmistress of Fortuna. And I have crucial evidence."

"It's a little late for new evidence," McCoy said. "The girl's been convicted and sentenced already. So if you could *kindly* leave my home, maybe no one else will have to be arrested."

Mell's grip on the knife tightened.

"A conviction doesn't hold in the face of new evidence," Penelope said quickly.

"Look, little lady. It's the weekend. You can come to my office on Monday."

Penelope gritted her teeth. "You know perfectly well that it will be too late by then. You should also know that you *have* to accept new evidence."

The man frowned at her tone. "Says who?"

"Our lawyer," Penelope snarled, slapping a letter down on the table. Mell looked at her, surprised.

"Where did you get that?" she hissed under her breath.

"I like to be prepared," Penelope whispered.

McCoy skimmed the letter with a frown.

"Fine," he said tightly. "Florence, why don't you go wait in the other room?"

His wife rose stiffly from the table. She refused to even look at Mell as she passed by, but Mell stopped her with the tip of the knife she still held.

"If the sheriff comes banging on the door while we're talking, I might get trigger happy. So, probably best to just go into the next room as the judge asked, and keep your mouth shut."

With a gulp, the woman hurried from the room.

"There is no need to threaten my wife!" McCoy snapped.

"Really? When you're planning on murdering my sister?"

"As your *lawyer* must have explained to you, Miss Currier, a lawful execution is far from murder."

"What about hanging an innocent girl when you know she committed no crime?" Mell asked.

"Two men of the law *saw* her do it."

"Not two," Penelope cut it, pressing her papers to the table in front of the judge.

McCoy looked down, startled. "What do you mean?"

"This," Penelope said, laying a finger on the paper, "is a receipt for a telegram that Deputy Lewis Greenman sent from Fortuna on the seventh of July."

The judge glanced down at the paper, then back up at Penelope. His face was blank. "So?"

"So, Mayor Bailey was shot on July seventh. Yet somehow Deputy Greenman was able to testify that he saw the mayor shot. In White Hills. Fifty miles from Fortuna."

The judge frowned over the paper. "Who wrote this receipt?"

"Postmaster Gillespie. He retired nine months ago, when I took over from him."

The judge hummed over that piece of information, his eyes tracing the pencil marks on the paper.

Then he lifted his eyes to Penelope again. "Perhaps the deputy left the message with the postmaster before riding out with the sheriff and his posse."

"To cover fifty miles, Sheriff Wiley must have left Fortuna in the early hours of the morning on the sixth of July, at the very latest. I don't know how long it's been, your honor, since you last sent a telegram yourself, instead of sending one of your clerks to do it for you, but the point of telegrams is that they are instantaneous. If you didn't mind your message arriving over twenty-four hours after you sent it, you'd save your coins and use the penny post."

Judge McCoy looked rankled, but his voice remained irritatingly calm—and condescending. "Well, then. It seems this Postmaster Gillespie—an old man from the looks of his hand, and on the brink of retirement—simply got his dates wrong."

Penelope curled her fingers into her palm, letting her nails bite into the tender flesh there, to force herself to stay as calm as the judge. "Perhaps," she allowed, as she pushed the second piece of paper closer to the judge. "But then, we'd have to believe that he got the date wrong on *this* telegram as well. It's the message that Deputy Greenman was replying to on the seventh. And you'll see, your honor, that it's clearly dated July sixth."

The judge opened his mouth, but Penelope cut him off.

"*And*, we'd then have to assume he got the date wrong on this one, as well." She slapped a third slip of paper down on the dark mahogany.

It was a reply from Lewis's mother, which had come in late in the day on the seventh of July, thanking Lewis for his message "this morning" and telling him that his father was unfortunately worse than ever. "Are you prepared to impugn the professional honor of Postmaster Gillespie to *that* degree, your honor?"

McCoy bristled. "This is hardly the kind of evidence that will let a known murderer walk." He brushed the papers back across the table toward Penelope. "A few telegrams, against the testimony of a man of the law?"

Mell's hand flew to the revolver that sat at her hip. "What do you mean?" she demanded. "The deputy *clearly* lied."

"A conviction has to stand beyond a reasonable doubt," Penelope said quickly. "That's what the lawyer said. If this evidence isn't enough to exonerate Corinna, it certainly introduces a 'reasonable doubt.'"

McCoy hesitated.

"One we'd also be happy to take to the newspapers, and to the governor."

McCoy sighed heavily. "Fine." He pointed a meaty finger at Mell. "You have that lawyer of yours get on the next train from Tucson. We'll talk about this man-to-man on Monday."

"And the execution?" Penelope pressed.

"Will be held until we can sort this mess out." He narrowed his eyes. "But don't get your hopes up. I'm sure we'll have plenty of witnesses willing to say that Deputy Greenman was here in White Hills that day, and plenty more willing to testify that your postmaster got his dates wrong."

Penelope swallowed hard. Was that all it would take? Would Wiley just need to get a few more of his pals to lie for him?

"Thank you," Penelope said tightly. "No need to see us out."

The judge's wife was hovering anxiously in the doorway of the parlor when they stalked out of the room. She gave a squeak.

"Mrs. McCoy," Penelope said with a nod. "Sorry to ruin your breakfast."

Out on the street, Mell burst out angrily, "That condescending son of a bitch! He's going to 'sort out this mess,' all right, by covering it up!"

"Mell..." Penelope tried.

"No, librarian." Mell shook her head. She reached up to cup Penelope's face. "You did your best. That fake letter from the lawyer was really smart. But you're trying too hard to play by the rules. Men like that? They make the rules; they don't follow them."

"But we got the stay of execution."

"For how long? He's probably burning those papers as we speak. She'll go to the gallows on Tuesday instead of Monday."

Penelope reached out to grip her arms. "Then that gives us one more day."

Mell gave a soft, sad laugh. "You are so optimistic," she said. "What's one day going to do?"

"We can try to find more evidence. We know what happened now. There must be someone who saw Wiley shoot the mayor!"

"Even if someone did, you think anyone is going to be willing to testify against him? To help someone like Corinna?"

"But it's the right thing to do!"

"Not everyone's as good as you, librarian," Mell said. They stepped up to the carriage.

"What happened?" Vera demanded, taking in the expressions on their faces.

"We're going to get my sister," Mell said, climbing onto the front of the carriage.

"Mell!"

"No, Penelope. We're done playing by their rules. We do what's *right*, not what the law says. And you and I both know that Corinna didn't do anything wrong. So bustin' her out of jail is the *right* thing to do."

Penelope hesitated. Knowing that the law wasn't always right didn't make it right to go in with guns blazing. Two things could be wrong at the same time.

"Corinna will be a wanted murderer for the rest of her life. Is that really what you want?"

Mell gave her a wry grin. "The whole crew's wanted for something."

"Yeah," Penelope scoffed. "But you all actually committed those crimes. Corinna didn't do this. Do you want her to be looking over her shoulder every day for the rest of her life?"

That gave Mell pause. "She's just a kid, Penelope. She's sitting in that jail cell, all alone, expecting to die. I have to do *something*."

Penelope didn't know what to say to that.

In her silence, Mell pulled her pistol free, checking it was fully loaded. Penelope scrambled up on the box next to her.

"Mell, people are going to *die*."

"Yes, they are. Every man who stand between me and my sister."

The carriage burst into life, heading for the prison.

She understood Mell's position—she knew that a lifetime of bitter disappointments meant that the captain wasn't willing to trust in the system and hope for the best. But she also knew that a shoot-out in the streets of White Hills had gotten them into this trouble in the first place. How would repeating their mistakes make things better?

She cast her eyes out over the road, hoping desperately for an idea. She searched the faces of the people they passed, wondering if they would get hurt in the coming melee. Would that man grab his rifle and come running when shots started ringing out? Would that woman get hit?

She scanned the crowds, and then almost tumbled off the box of the carriage in surprise. "*Lewis*?" she gasped.

There, looking lost in the hubbub of the street, was Lewis Greenman.

"Stop the carriage!" she shouted to Mell, already scrambling off.

"Penelope!" Mell called, but the carriage hissed to a stop.

"Lewis!" Penelope yelled, as soon as her feet hit the ground.

Lewis stopped in the middle of the road, looking behind himself in confusion.

"Lewis Greenman," Penelope called, and watched him tense all over. He looked up at Mell on the box of the carriage and quivered.

"Miss Moser?" Unable to hide, Lewis slunk toward them.

"What on earth are you doing here?" Penelope asked when he was near enough.

"I could ask you the same thing, Miss Moser. I thought you were in Fortuna."

Penelope darted a glance back to the carriage. "I got a ride with friends."

Lewis followed her gaze and paled. "I see."

"I thought you were in Yuma," Penelope countered.

"I—" He stared down at his boots. "I couldn't stop thinking about what you said."

"What did you say?" Mell asked, jumping down beside Penelope.

Lewis startled like a rabbit, clearly wishing Mell was a million miles away, but he forged on, doggedly. "About guilt. About living with what I've done. I—" He shot a nervous glance at Mell, and the hand she had tucked behind her back. "I never thought anyone was getting hurt," he admitted with a gulp. "I never thought about the girl at all." He steeled himself, squeezing his eyes shut tight before looking determinedly at Mell.

"I'm sorry," Lewis said. "Miss Moser called her—your, um, sister—a young girl. And I just never thought... Well, I never thought past what Sheriff Wiley said."

That she was a hussy, a harlot, a monster. Penelope knew. She'd heard it all.

"She may be a criminal," Lewis continued, determined. "But no one should ever be hung for what they didn't do. That's not justice. And what I signed up for was justice." His hand went to the badge on his chest, slightly grimy and tarnished, but still reflecting flecks of the morning sun.

"Lewis Greenman," Penelope said with a smile. "I always knew you were the best of the whole Fortuna lot."

Lewis flushed, scuffing his boot toe in the red dirt. "Aw, Miss Moser."

"Now, let's get you in front of the judge."

Lewis's eyebrows rose. "Now?"

Penelope stepped forward, snagging his arm. "What did you come to White Hills for, if not to see to the judge?"

"Yes, but—" Lewis balked as Mell stepped up to grab his other arm. "What am I supposed to say?"

"The truth, Lewis," Penelope said, her heart buoying. "I've heard it sets you free."

Between the two of them, they just about frog-marched Lewis back to Judge McCoy's house. Penelope could see why Wiley had wanted him. Lewis was easily led. But he'd gotten on the train to White Hills on his own, and that was what really mattered.

As they came up to the house again, Penelope could see the face of the serving girl pressed to the window. Her skin was dead white.

The door was bolted against them.

Mell hammered on the door. "We don't want no trouble," she called. "But we need to see the judge again."

"He's heard your testimony already," a male voice answered.

"We've got new testimony," Mell yelled, giving the door an extra thump for good measure. Between them, Lewis jumped.

"In the last five minutes?"

"Yes!"

There was a long silence, and then they heard a key turn in the lock. The door swung open, and Judge McCoy himself peered out. He appeared ready for a fight, but then his gaze landed on Lewis and his eyes widened.

"My star witness," he said, clearly at a loss.

"Your honor, sir," Lewis mumbled, his face red.

"These, um, ladies troubling you, boy?"

Lewis stood up straighter, squaring his shoulders. "No, sir. I got some testimony to give."

The judge looked between the three of them and shook his head slowly, but stepped back to allow them inside.

Lewis told his story in a rush, while the judge paced his parlor. How Wiley planned the ambush to catch the gang when their guard was down. How Wiley told him to stay behind in Fortuna because he "wasn't worth a damn" in a fight. How Wiley didn't tell him anything about the shoot-out, except that "those bitches got what was coming to them," until two weeks later, when Wiley demanded he come to White Hills to testify. Even then Wiley didn't want to tell him what really happened in White Hills that day; he just expected Lewis to take the stand and parrot back whatever Wiley wanted him to say. But Lewis was a truthful man, and he wasn't ready to lie in a court of law that easily.

That was when Wiley admitted he'd shot the mayor, firing at what he thought was one of the bandits, and only then realizing what he'd done.

"And what? He deliberately set up this girl?" McCoy demanded.

"He wanted to say that Mirage Currier had done it," Lewis said, sneaking a peek at Mell, who stood tensely in the corner of the room, listening to his story. "He wanted her to hang most of all. But one of the other men testified to the fact that Currier was holed up in the bank for nearly all of the fight. So then Wiley had to change his plan. He asked around, seeing what girl he could pin it on. And Corinna Currier was the only one unaccounted for during the shoot-out."

"That's because she wasn't involved in it!" Mell spat out.

"And why did you go along with this, son?"

"Wiley said his career would be ruined. A lawman taken off the streets, all for the sake of a—" He shot another glance at Mell.

"Go on," she said icily.

"A two-bit whore, who wasn't worth the rope she'd swing on," Lewis whispered, staring down at his shoes. "So I lied. I said I was there when I wasn't, and I said I saw things that never really happened."

"Well. That changes an awful lot," McCoy said, stricken. He sat down heavily in a chair. Penelope and Mell watched him with bated breath. Finally, he let out a huff. "There's nothing else for it," he said, almost to himself.

Mell reached out, snagging Penelope's hand and clutching it tight.

The judge looked up at them. "I'm officially overturning Corinna Currier's sentence."

Mell let out a wild whoop.

Penelope gasped. "Thank you, your honor."

"Don't thank me. I'm not doing it for you, or for anybody else. It's just the law. Thomas!"

A valet slunk nervously into the room, his eyes fixed warily on Mell. "Yes, sir?"

"I need you to take a note over to Sheriff Wood. He'll be at home this morning." McCoy got some paper from the writing desk by the window and dashed off a few lines.

"Yes, sir." The man hurried from the room, and McCoy turned back to Mell.

"You'll be able to pick her up this morning," he said.

Mell squeezed Penelope's hand like it was the only thing keeping her upright. "Thank you, sir." Her voice trembled.

"And Sheriff Barnett?" Penelope pressed. Across the room, Lewis flinched.

"Well, now," McCoy said, rubbing his chin. "I guess I'm going to have to issue a warrant for his arrest." He shook his head. "Manslaughter. Perjury. Conspiracy."

"I'd add reckless endangerment too, your honor," Penelope said. At the judge's startled expression, she continued, "Starting a gunfight in a crowded town without provocation?"

"Yes, thank you, Miss Moser," he said stiffly. "And, ambush or no, I'd rather not see any of you around White Hills again, is that clear?"

"Don't worry, sir," Mell said. "I think we've had more'n enough of this town."

They turned to leave, but the judge called them back. "Deputy Greenman, I need a few more words with you."

Lewis turned back, shrinking under the weight of the judge's gaze. "Am I in trouble?"

"Son, you committed perjury in a conspiracy to send an innocent party to the gallows."

Lewis's head hung.

"He also provided vital testimony against a far more dangerous man," Penelope said.

"I've had just about enough of your law speak, little lady," McCoy snapped. Then he sighed. "I'm not going to arrest him, all right? But I do need to give him a talking to about what it means to actually *uphold* the law."

"Well, that's all right, then," Penelope said, reaching out to pat Lewis on the shoulder. "Thank you, Lewis," she whispered.

"I'm real sorry about all this, Miss Moser."

"I know you are." Penelope snuck a peek at Mell, who hovered impatiently by the door. "We'll make you the same deal McCoy's given us—you keep your nose clean, and the *Star* will give Fortuna a wide berth. All right?"

"Yes, ma'am," Lewis agreed fervently. "We'll miss you all the same, Miss Moser," he added.

"Thanks, Lewis." She turned to the door, leaving the last piece of Fortuna behind her.

XIX.

The air in the carriage was tense as the prison came into view. It wasn't a large building. Lawless as the Wild West was, most outlaws wound up dead in the streets, not behind bars. From the outside, the building was hardly imposing. But the three women with Penelope had spent the last year of their lives locked up inside the squat, ugly structure. It was no wonder the sight of it set them on edge. Penelope knew Mell only half-believed that they'd let Corinna out without a fight. Her hand kept twitching to the gun on her hip as the carriage rolled down the dusty street.

"It's going to be fine," Penelope whispered, catching hold of those fingers and twining them with hers.

The carriage came to an abrupt halt, and Ruth let out a holler from the box. "I can see her!"

They all were at the window in a flash. Two men stood on the porch of the prison, flanking a third slender figure. But she wasn't shackled and they weren't holding on to her. She was a free woman.

"Oh my God," Mell whispered, fumbling for the door. Penelope reached across her and pulled the handle, letting Mell spill out. "*Corinna.*"

The girl shot out from between the guards, racing over to Mell.

"Oh God. You're okay," Mell said, rushing forward. They met in the middle of the road, wrapping each other up tight in their arms.

Vera, Penelope, and Ruth followed behind at a more sedate pace, giving the sisters a moment.

Corinna looked so *young*. That was all Penelope could focus on as the sisters embraced. She looked tired, and ragged, and so, so young.

She had brown eyes, the same color as Mell's, but bigger and framed with long, dark lashes that made her look younger than her eighteen years. The dress she wore hung on her. It was presumably the one she'd been arrested in, but now she was little more than skin and bones, and the fabric billowed loosely over her narrow frame. She was taller than Mell—then again, who wasn't?—but the height just made her look more frail, like a reed bending in a buffeting wind.

"Mell, what on earth is going on?" Corinna gasped, still clinging tight to her sister. "When you said you'd get me out, I thought you meant with guns blazin'. But they told me I been 'found innocent'!"

"You have. They know you didn't do it. They know you didn't do *anything*," Mell assured her.

"But how? You been saying that from day one, but they weren't listening."

"Got real, concrete evidence this time."

"But how?" Corinna asked again, pulling back from Mell to marvel at her. Her hair was lighter than Mell's, the color of straw in the late-summer sun. It hung in tangles down her back, nearly to her waist. The sight of her and all her delicate edges made Penelope's heart ache.

"Found someone who knew a thing or two about what really happened at the shooting." She nodded to Penelope. "Smart as a whip. Got the whole thing overturned."

"Mell," Penelope protested, her cheeks heating. But she stepped forward and extended a hand. "Penelope Moser. It's a pleasure to meet you, Corinna."

Corinna cut a look at Mell. "A real *lady*," she whispered with a giggle, but she took Penelope's hand, giving it a firm pump up and down. "Are you our newest recruit, then?" she asked.

"Yes," Penelope said, with no hesitation whatsoever.

Corinna's sunny smile was back. It lit her up, radiating warmth at whomever she turned it on. "Well. Welcome aboard," she said happily. "I hope Mell told you it's mostly washing dishes, misreading maps, and scrubbing the deck, rather than saving damsels from the gallows."

"I'm glad to hear it, to be honest," Penelope said, matching Corinna's grin. "I've had a *lot* of excitement over the last few days. Washing dishes sounds like a positive relief."

"I'm holding you to that, Moser," Vera said, stepping forward to fold Corinna into her arms. Ruth lumbered after her, wrapping them both up tight.

"I would have clobbered every one of 'un if they had actually tried to hang you," Ruth promised.

"Vera, are you crying?" Corinna asked.

"No," Vera denied through her tears.

"We've all been a bit beside ourselves," Mell admitted. "Even Vera."

"They've been on a rampage across the territory," Penelope said mildly. Corinna's head whipped toward her, interest shining in her eyes.

"Really?"

"Oh yes," Penelope said, ignoring Mell's wide eyes. "They kidnapped me *and* had a huge shoot-out in Fortuna."

Corinna's head swung back around to her sister. "You *kidnapped her*? Mell! There are easier ways to meet women!"

"Oh, hush, you," Mell grumbled. "There were *circumstances*. It all made sense at the time."

Corinna snickered. "I knew the *Star* would go to ruin without me."

Mell burrowed in between Vera and Ruth, squeezing her sister so tight the girl gave a little yelp. "*It has,*" she said fiercely.

Penelope felt tears sting her eyes as she looked at the little group. The wound that Corinna's absence had left was apparent to her, now. Fresh on the ship, she hadn't been able to read the signs, to see the clear outline of the girl that should have been there. But now it was obvious. Every member of the *Star*'s crew had been grieving.

"Let's get you home," Mell said after a moment.

"The *Star* is just outside town," Vera promised, pulling Corinna toward the carriage.

A ragged breath ripped out of Corinna, and Penelope turned to see tears on the girl's cheeks. "I never thought I'd see it again," Corinna murmured, tears falling freely.

"I would never have let them hang you," Mell promised fiercely.

"The *Star* always saves those who need saving," Penelope said, thinking how much braver and freer she was since meeting Mell. Byrdie, Elsie, Ruth, Vera, Penelope—they had all been saved by Mell, just as much as Corinna had. And Corinna had saved them too.

Corinna turned her head, smiling brilliantly at Penelope. "I think I'm gonna like you."

"Thank you," Penelope whispered.

Taking in a shaky breath, Mell gave Corinna a little push toward the carriage. "Enough of this sappy nonsense," she said, as if she didn't have tears glistening on her cheeks. "Let's go home."

"Yes, please," Corinna said fervently.

The mood on the *Star* was euphoric. The crew crowded Corinna, passing her from arms to arms.

"We missed you," Elsie cried.

"It was awful without you," Byrdie assured her.

"Thank God," June kept repeating, tucking Corinna against her breast and raising fervent eyes to the heavens.

Penelope really understood then that they were more than a crew; they were a family, and she was finally seeing it complete. Then Mell reached out to tug her into the fray, and Penelope figured they might be a family with room for one more.

"And thank God for Penelope," June said, catching sight of her and extending an arm to sweep her into the embrace.

"I barely did anything!" she protested.

"Except outsmarting every last man in White Hills," Mell crowed.

"It was Lewis who got her released in the end," Penelope insisted.

"And who got him to talk?"

Penelope's cheeks heated, but she insisted, "Thank God for Lewis Greenman's change of heart."

"We don't cheer a lot of men on this ship," Vera muttered dubiously, but the other women took up the call.

"To Lewis Greenman!" echoed throughout the cabin. It was probably the most credit the poor deputy had ever gotten in his life. Penelope wished he could have heard it, for all he'd be a nervous wreck if he found himself on the *Persephone Star*. He deserved to be cheered, though, and she wasn't sure what kind of reception was going to greet him back in Fortuna, not when the White Hills lawmen were coming for Wiley.

"We should have a party!" Byrdie cried.

"For Lewis?" Ruth asked, perplexed.

"For Corinna!" Byrdie chided with a laugh.

"Yes, for Corinna!" The cry went up from the whole group.

"Get us the hell out of White Hills first, Byrdie," Mell said.

"And then?" Byrdie asked, her impish eyes twinkling.

"And then a party," Mell allowed, and the group cheered again.

Byrdie scampered off for the deck, to fly them far away from the town that had caused them so much trouble.

"Where will we go?" Penelope asked Mell, while the rest of the crew still enveloped Corinna.

"Anywhere we want," she said with a shrug.

The idea of it was equal parts exciting and terrifying. Penelope had moved an awful lot in her life, chasing Ashes as he chased money. But she'd never gotten a say in where they went. They followed the gold and the hardships that succeeded it. Now, the road in front of her was wide open. Even the sky wasn't the limit on the *Star*. More importantly, she was beginning to realize there was a difference between the *Star*'s roaming and Ashes's. Wherever the *Star* went, its crew was still home. That was what had been missing from Penelope's for the last fifteen years, since her mother had died and they left New York.

XX.

The ship was a whirlwind of activity. Byrdie brought them about-face, and steered them south, toward Mexico. Penelope had never been beyond the territories, and her heart leapt at the idea of something new.

The rest of the crew set about throwing a party. Vera headed to the kitchen to rustle up some food, while Ruth brought whiskey from the storeroom, and Elsie put a record on the gramophone. The lights sparkled and the music seemed to carry all the women up off their feet.

"Dancing!" Elsie cried, clapping her hands.

A cheer went up from the group, and then all the women jostled with each other to lead Corinna in the first dance. She giggled, her face flushed pink, before finally allowing Elsie to sweep her onto the floor. Ruth held out a solemn hand to June, who surprised Penelope by assenting and allowing herself to be led to the center of the mess. The song was upbeat, and the dancers launched into the Portland; Corinna and Elsie were very competent, their feet flying over the floor. Ruth was clumsier, but June maintained perfect dignity as the larger woman led her haltingly around the room.

"Pretty good." Byrdie laughed. "But I reckon we can teach them a thing or two, whaddya think, Vera?"

"If you can keep up," Vera said. They galloped onto the floor, literally dancing circles around the other couples.

"Librarian?" Mell asked, raising an eyebrow.

"It would be my pleasure," Penelope said. Mell pulled her into the center of the room, a wide grin on her face.

Penelope had been to her share of dances, so she knew the steps, even though the lively group of women in the ship's mess was a far cry from the dances they had back east. It was more fun, though.

Mell was shorter than her, but a strong leader. Her hands were sure and firm at Penelope's waist, spinning her to the music. They moved faster and faster, Mell's face glowing pink, a broad smile on her face. Penelope tipped her head back with a laugh, watching the lights of the sconces twinkle across the ceiling.

"It's a good thing you stayed," Mell called over the music. "You balance our numbers."

"An important duty," Penelope said with mock gravitas. "I'll do my best to live up to it."

"So, ship's librarian, dance partner . . ." Mell said thoughtfully. "Any other jobs you'd like?"

"I'd like to try *everything*," Penelope said honestly. She'd had so little room for developing herself for anything other than marriage and motherhood, she had no idea what she'd like or what she'd be good at. Maybe she'd find she had an aptitude for mechanics, or mapmaking, or piloting the ship.

Mell grinned. "Everything it is," she agreed, twirling Penelope around the room.

Eventually Vera slipped away from the dancing, and in what felt like no time, she returned carrying a large platter. "If you heathens want to eat," she called over the music, "then you need to carry!"

A cheer went up at the sight of the food, and everyone clambered for the kitchen to carry out dish after dish. Mell circled the table, pouring a considerable dram of whiskey for each place setting.

"Oh, I couldn't," Penelope said with a laugh, trying to cover her glass with her hand.

Confusion furrowed Ruth's brow. "No whiskey?"

"Well, I've never . . ." Penelope began, and then wondered why. What was to stop her? It wasn't *ladylike*, but who cared about that?

"All right. Just a little!" Penelope said over the whoops of approval.

"A toast!" Mell called as they all took their places. Everyone lifted their glasses high in the air. "To family!"

"To family!"

"To home!" Corinna added, happiness shining in her eyes.

"To home!" they echoed, and Penelope felt like she'd never smiled wider in her life.

She raised the glass to her lips, inhaling the scent she normally associated with her father and his friends, and took a dainty sip.

She spluttered over the table.

Laughter rang round the table. Mell curled over her plate, pounding her fist on the table.

"Hey," Penelope choked out around the burn in her throat. "Was this supposed to be some kind of a trick?"

"No trick," Ruth said, holding up her own glass. "It's the same as what we're all drinking."

The other women lifted their own glasses in a toast to Penelope. She pursed her lips and wiped at the tears that had sprung to her eyes, but lifted her own glass. "Bottoms up, I suppose," she sighed.

A chorus of cheers went up.

"You don't really have to," Mell said, leaning forward across the table so she could drop her voice as the other women turned back to the plates and conversations. "You can sneak it into my glass if it don't suit you."

That warmed Penelope's belly more than the whiskey.

"No. I don't mind joining in. I'll just take little sips."

"All right." Mell leaned back, grinning. "You be careful with that stuff, now. It'll take you by surprise."

"Sneak up on me, will it?" Penelope laughed, raising the glass to her lips once more. It still burned, but a little less than last time.

Dinner passed and the whiskey got easier and easier to swallow. Before Penelope knew it, Elsie and Byrdie were clearing the plates away and she was staring into the bottom of an empty glass.

"We'll make a woman out of you yet." Vera laughed, tipping the bottle over her glass again.

Penelope smiled as the liquid chugged into her glass. It seemed to sparkle more in the low lamplight.

The dancing and drinking continued throughout the afternoon. After the first bottle of whiskey ran dry, Vera started singing, running through all the music hall favorites in a mellow, husky voice. After the second bottle was finished, June joined her, in a clear sweet voice that was meant for church hymns, not the saucy songs Vera knew. Hearing her bellow out "Ta-ra-ra Boom-de-ay!" brought the company to tears as they laughed and clapped along.

Almost unconsciously, Penelope's found her eyes drawn to Mell. The captain was easy and relaxed, head thrown back with laughter, limbs loose as she sprawled in her seat. Her hair was mussed, sweat shone on her brow, and she looked beautiful and happy and free. She was irresistible.

Penelope stood up so suddenly her chair scraped loudly against the wood floor.

"We need more whiskey," she announced, turning her eyes to Mell.

Mell's gaze slid to the unopened bottle in the middle of the table, and she raised an eyebrow. "We do?"

"Yes," Penelope said firmly.

"Okay," Mell agreed with a shrug, hauling herself up from her chair. She loped over to Penelope. "Lead the way."

The mess doors swung shut behind them, muffling the noise of the party. In the silence, Penelope's ears rung. "You're getting to be quite the libertine, librarian," Mell said.

Penelope blushed, not looking back at Mell as she strode down the passage. "Maybe."

The door to the storeroom was just ahead. Penelope took a deep breath and pushed it open.

Mell ambled into the small space behind her, her eyes already on the shelves. "You have any requests?" she asked. "A favorite tipple?"

Whiskey stirred the blood in Penelope's veins, giving her confidence. She stepped forward, grasped Mell by the shoulders, and bore her back until she hit the door.

"I didn't actually come in here for the booze," Penelope said, as Mell blinked up at her with surprised eyes.

"No?" The word came out a choked whisper.

"No," Penelope agreed, and leaned in. At the touch of their lips, everything seemed to go quiet, except for the blood pounding in her ears.

Mell's mouth was warm and soft. Her lips parted and Penelope tasted the sting of whiskey that lingered on her tongue. She curled her fingers into Mell's shirt, crowding closer until the outline of Mell's body pressed against hers. She swayed, dizzy with sensation. She kissed Mell like it was the only thing keeping her steady. Like her life depended on it.

"*Librarian*," Mell whispered into her mouth, sounding half-shocked. Her hands slid slowly down the length of Penelope's body, leaving fire in their wake. Penelope trembled. Mell's touch was a brand, even through too many layers of cotton. Penelope wanted her closer, and closer, and closer. She canted her hips forward and Mell hungrily pushed back. Suddenly Mell was everywhere, her hands all over Penelope: on her back, on her hips. Penelope felt like she was going to shatter into a thousand pieces.

"Is this just the whiskey?" Mell panted, but she kept her hands on Penelope.

"No," Penelope murmured, setting her mouth to Mell's neck, dragging her lips down the column of flesh. Mell shuddered in her arms. "I've just decided to be brave."

Mell tipped her head back to bark out a laugh. "You've been brave since the second I met you."

Penelope nipped at the pale flesh between her teeth, wrenching a groan from Mell. "Then it must be something about you."

"No," Mell said, reaching up to cradle Penelope's face. "It most certainly is not."

Pressed together, Mell's heart beat fiercely alongside her own. "I'm glad you kidnapped me."

That drew another laugh. "Better tell Ruth or she'll feel guilty till the end of time."

Penelope knew they should go back to the party. She didn't begrudge it. She knew this was allowed now. Whenever she wanted she could pull Mell aside and kiss her. It made her feel so free and powerful, she was pretty sure she could take on the world.

"Come on," she said, darting in to brush one more kiss over Mell's pliant mouth. "We have celebrating to do."

The noise of the party met them as they opened the door, and Mell shot her a grin before tangling their fingers together and leading the way back to the din.

Father,

I hear that Wiley has been arrested. I don't hold what he did against you in any way. You couldn't have known. I want to thank you for the support you gave me growing up, and to let you know that I've finally found my place in the world. I'm happy, I promise.

If you keep your business clean, you won't ever have anything to fear from the Persephone Star. *And who knows? Maybe one day we'll all be together again, and you can see what it's like to sail through the skies.*

Always your loving daughter,
Penelope

Dear Reader,

Thank you for reading Jamie Sullivan's *The Persephone Star*!

We know your time is precious and you have many, many entertainment options, so it means a lot that you've chosen to spend your time reading. We really hope you enjoyed it.

We'd be honored if you'd consider posting a review—good or bad—on sites like **Amazon, Barnes & Noble, Kobo, Goodreads, Twitter, Facebook, Tumblr,** and your blog or website. We'd also be honored if you told your friends and family about this book. Word of mouth is a book's lifeblood!

For more information on upcoming releases, author interviews, blog tours, contests, giveaways, and more, please sign up for our weekly, spam-free newsletter and visit us around the web:

Newsletter: riptidepublishing.com/newsletter
Twitter: twitter.com/RiptideBooks
Facebook: facebook.com/RiptidePublishing
Goodreads: tinyurl.com/RiptideOnGoodreads
Tumblr: riptidepublishing.tumblr.com

Thank you so much for Reading the Rainbow!

RiptidePublishing.com

ALSO BY JAMIE SULLIVAN

Heart of the Dragon
The Only Way
Imaginary
Prom and Other Hazards
Enter the Dragon
Fumbling Towards Crescendo

ABOUT THE AUTHOR

Jamie Sullivan has been writing for what feels like her entire life—her parents' attic is full of notebooks brimming with early attempts at fiction. She's found her stride, however, in romance. She's happy experimenting with genre, and has written supernatural, science fiction, and realist stories.

Catch up with her at jamiesullivanbooks.wordpress.com or on Twitter @jsullivanwrites.

Enjoy more stories like
The Persephone Star
at RiptidePublishing.com!

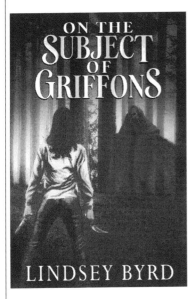

On the Subject of Griffons

They'll do anything to save their children's lives, even if it means working together.

ISBN: 978-1-62649-883-9

Bound with Love

A perfect life—until one letter threatens to unravel it all.

ISBN: 978-1-62649-263-9

Printed in Poland
by Amazon Fulfillment
Poland Sp. z o.o., Wrocław

58551852R00113